THE TUTOR

DANIEL HURST

www.danielhurstbooks.com

'Tell me and I forget. Teach me and I remember.'

Benjamin Franklin

THE FIRST LESSON

The glow from the flames could be seen for miles.

At a distance, they might have looked beautiful. But up close, they weren't quite so pretty. They roared, raced and devoured every part of the building and soon there was nothing left of the school.

This place where so many children sat exams was no match for the test it faced that night. In the morning, only ash and embers remained, and unless you were from this area, then you wouldn't even know that a school had been here at all. But if you were from this town, then you will have known about the devastation that occurred here.

A place where youngsters learnt, a place where adults taught, and a place where the first shoots of promising careers grew. All gone, wiped out in a blaze as unforgiving as a bad grade or a detention. By the time the sun came up on this

Warwickshire town, there was no school and nowhere for the children to learn.

Forget Maths, English and Science.

The first lesson is that every action has consequences.

1

AMY

I always hated school. The sight of all the uniforms descending on one location. The sound of the bell blaring out across the playground. The smell of disinfectant in the corridors, as if that would be enough to prevent the spread of germs in a place full of snotty children. And worst of all, the feeling of dread in my stomach as I passed through the gates on my way to another day of classes.

Thank God I don't have to go through that anymore. Thank God I am the parent now, instead of the pupil.

I can still see all the uniforms around me, just like I can hear the bell ringing out across this concrete playground. I'm sure that if I walked inside and stood in the corridors, then I would smell the bleach too. But it doesn't seem as bad now because I know that I am only here for a few minutes. Even the feeling of dread in my stomach is only a fraction of what it once was as I pass through the gates today. Maybe that's because I'm older and wiser, or maybe it's just because I'm driving through them in my car rather than shuffling through them by foot with my heavy schoolbag. Either way, being back here again isn't as bad as it used to be for me. But that doesn't mean that I like it. I still can't wait to drop my kids off and get out of here. This place gives me the jitters.

It always has, and it always will.

As I head towards one of the few remaining spaces in the car park, navigating my vehicle through a sea of riotous youngsters and sleep-deprived parents, I am struck again by how much this place has changed since I was a pupil here. The uniform is still the same rancid purple colour that it always was, the bell still carries its eardrum-bursting volume, and the school gates still cause butterflies, but everything else is different. The drab grey building has gone, in its place a gleaming metallic structure that looks a lot more appealing than the premises where I spent so much of my childhood. The car park is bigger and better maintained now and not the pothole-ridden mess that it was when I used to navigate it as a child. And in the distance, I can see the fences that circle the sports pitches, all very modern and state-of-the-art and a far cry from the patch of gravel where I used to have to play hockey while trying to avoid falling over and losing half of the skin on my legs.

There is no doubt about it. This place looks a lot better than it used to.

Maybe the fire wasn't such a bad thing to happen after all...

I shake my head as if to brush away the memory of the inferno before it can entrench itself further into my day. It was a long time ago, and things have moved on. These school grounds are evidence of that.

'Mum, watch out!'

The sound of my son's voice from behind me in the back seat snaps me out of my daydream, and I slam on the brakes just before I hit the mother and child walking across the front of our car.

I wave an apologetic hand at the passing parent who scowls at me as she leads her daughter away from my vehicle. I was only going five miles an hour, but still, best not to bump into the pupils at any speed. That sort of thing could lead to the Headmaster issuing me with a ban from parking here which would be annoying for the school run. My daughter Bella is in her first year at Sharpbell High, so I'm a long way off leaving this place behind for good.

'Good driving,' says my son, Michael, and I roll my eyes at his sarcasm.

'Let me know when you pass your test, and then you can comment,' I reply, and that shuts him up.

At sixteen, he is still a year off being able to begin driving lessons, which means he is still a long way from being ready to get behind the wheel and drive himself around. He hates the fact that I still drop him off, although I have told him that he is more than welcome to get the bus or walk instead. Of course, he doesn't do either of those things because that would require him having to get out of bed earlier in the morning and he can't bear the thought of doing that.

I guide my car into the parking spot and relax, having successfully navigated my way through the minefield that is the school grounds at half-past eight on a Monday morning.

'Thanks Mum,' Bella says as she picks up her bag from the footwell and opens her door.

'Have a good day love,' I say to her, but she is already out, eager to get inside and see her friends. She actually likes going to school, which is something that neither Michael nor I could ever say.

'Good luck with your test,' I say to my son as he begrudgingly gathers up his belongings and forces himself out into the real world.

He grunts back a response and then slams the door shut, which was nothing less than I expected. He's hardly been the best conversationalist since he entered his teens and things aren't likely to improve now that he is in the final year of school and facing the dreaded GCSE's. Like I was at his age, he hates life and can't wait to leave the world of classrooms, teachers and homework behind. He doesn't know what he wants to do after his exams, but I'm trying not to worry about him. I am sure that he will figure it out, just like I did. The important thing is that he knuckles down and gets good grades because that will give him more options when he does finally decide on what he wants to do.

As I watch my offspring walk away in opposite directions across the car park, I smile at how different the pair of them are. Bella is almost skipping across the concrete as she heads for class, whereas Michael is moving like he is walking through mud. I'll miss these times when they are gone.

But I won't miss this place.

Satisfied with another successful school run, I fiddle with the rear-view mirror and prepare to reverse out of this spot and get home. But before I put my car back into motion, I catch sight of my reflection in the mirror and notice the bags under my eyes and the line of wrinkles on my forehead. I never put makeup on to do the school run, but perhaps I should start. I look like something that has crawled out of a tomb. Okay, maybe not that bad, but I'm hardly looking my best. I'm only forty, but the reflection in the mirror has me looking older.

As I reverse out and head for the school gates, I find myself feeling a little envious of all the youthful faces that pass me by. But then I remember where they are going and what they are going to be doing all day and that envy turns into a smug satisfaction.

They have to go and listen to some boring old fart teaching them about grammar, Periodic Tables and tectonic plates, whereas I am on my way home to put my feet up and have a cup of tea.

I'd rather be forty than fourteen, that's for sure.

2

MICHAEL

I hate my life.

I'm sitting at the back of a classroom listening to some boring old fart wittering on about tectonic plates, and I have no idea why I need to know about any of this. I live in the middle of England. While there are a lot of problems here, earthquakes aren't one of them. Nor do I have any ambition of having a career in geology. So why am I being forced to listen to this spiel about subduction? Why am I being forced to listen to an old guy who I have nothing in common with?

And why is that old guy now looking right at me?

'Sorry, what?' I say, suddenly aware that all eyes in the class are on me. I've obviously just been asked a question, but I have no idea what it was.

'How do you expect to pass your exams if you don't pay attention?' Mr Reynolds asks me, with the smug superiority that all my teachers seem to possess.

'I'll be fine on the day,' I reply, which gets a few chuckles from my classmates around the room.

'The results of your mock exams say otherwise,' Mr Reynolds snaps back, instantly cutting me down and letting everybody here know that I'm not actually as clever as I am pretending to be right now.

I resist the urge to say anything else, even though I have several comebacks that I could use to get another laugh from my audience. But that would be pointless because it would probably just end with me being put in detention again and I don't want that. I just need to get through these next few months. Then I will be free.

No more school. No more teachers. No more learning about things that will have no bearing on the rest of my life.

Mr Reynolds goes back to his textbook, but my attention drifts to the window, where I look out over the empty playground and at the sports fields in the distance. I can't wait to leave this place behind. I can't wait to see something other than these walls and that concrete and those pitches.

I just need to be patient. I just need to get through my exams.

Then all of this will be over.

3

AMY

It's good to be back home. Fighting my way through the morning rush hour is a staple of my week, but now it is time for another one. A cup of tea and a slice of toast. And not an angry motorist in sight.

Bliss.

Sitting down on the sofa and grabbing the remote, I turn the television on but make sure to keep the volume low so as not to disturb my husband in the other room. Nick and I have been married for eighteen years, and he has been working from home for ten of them. It suits him because he doesn't have to commute and it suits me because it means I get to see him whenever I want to, although I try not to disturb him too much. He has an important job, although I can't even pretend to understand the complexity of it. He works in I.T. and can fix his client's server issues remotely, but that's about all I know. It sounds very technical and geeky, and his desk is full of huge textbooks about different software systems and such, which he seems to enjoy, but I just find confusing and dull. He's a clever man, certainly much smarter than me, which is why he is fixing somebody's computer problems right now while I'm eating a piece of toast and watching This Morning.

The good thing about I.T., at least from my perspective, is that it pays very well, which means I only have to work part-time in my own employment. I do two days a week at an office in town and get paid a pittance for it, but it gives me a change of scene and gives me my own income to spend on little luxuries. There's no stress in filing a few papers and listening to the girls in the office gossip about what they watched on television the night before, and I'm happy to do it, even if we would be fine on Nick's wage alone. But today is one of my days off so it's feet up and time to relax.

With the kids at school all day, and my husband beavering away in the study until I interrupt him with a cup of tea later, I am free to do whatever I like. That sounds like I have many options but considering it's raining outside and it's only Monday morning, there isn't actually that much to do. I'll probably put a wash on later.

Go me.

But it is nice to have this time to myself. It didn't always used to be this way. I haven't always had a lovely family, home and so much free time. I used to be just as unequipped for life as Michael is going to be.

I find myself worrying about my son even with the tea, toast and TV to distract me. The results of his mock exams last month were dreadful, even worse than the grades I got in my school days, which is saying something. It's not that he doesn't have the brains to succeed; it's just that he isn't applying himself. The string of detentions and letters from school is evidence of that. I don't like to call my son a troublemaker, but I'm afraid that seems to be what he is. I know he isn't like that because he is genuinely a nuisance, but rather because he is bored. Nick has spoken to him several times about the importance of working hard over the next few months and leaving school with good grades, but

Michael doesn't seem to take it on board, and their talks usually end up in an argument. That's because they are so different. Nick is happy to sit in a room all day with a laptop and a pile of paperwork, but Michael isn't. He wants to be outside being active and getting himself as far away from anything that resembles work as possible.

I have tried speaking to my son about it too. After all, I was exactly like him at his age. I was forever in detention and forever being told by my parents that I needed to stop messing around and knuckle down with my studies. It's only with hindsight that I can see they were right. There is no doubt that I would have avoided so much of the stresses that accompanied my late teens and early twenties if only I had focused more at school and given myself options after leaving. As it was, I spent several years bouncing about between various dead-end jobs, never really having the direction, drive or finances to change my life for the better. I'm sure I would have turned out just fine even if I hadn't been with Nick, although there is no question that I wouldn't have been able to work part-time and live in a house like this without him.

Money isn't the be-all and end-all of life, and real happiness comes from family and friendships, which I am so grateful to have. But I want my son to be comfortable when he is older and having a good job will see to that. He might not care about having the money for a house and a holiday now, but he will do one day.

But by then, it might be too late.

I turn off the television because I can't concentrate on what is happening on the screen. My mind is running away with itself again, as it likes to do on several occasions, and the only way to snap myself out of it when I am like this is to go and talk to Nick. He always knows what to say to make everything alright. But I also want to discuss something with him. It's the same thing we have spoken about before, although we haven't come to a final decision on it. It's the thing that I know Michael will hate in the short term but might be for the best in the long term.

It's the idea of hiring our son a personal tutor.

4

MICHAEL

Lunchtime. The only part of the school day that I enjoy. I am free to run around in the fresh air and kick a ball about for the next hour without anybody asking me a question or giving me homework. I'm going to enjoy it while I can.

'Pass!' I shout to Nev, who is my best friend but a terrible football player. Unfortunately, Nev fails to do as I say and he gets tackled, losing the ball and gifting the other team with an easy goal.

'Sorry mate,' he says sheepishly as I jog past him and I can't help but smile. He isn't rubbish at football on purpose; he just doesn't have much of a natural aptitude for the game. Fortunately, I am a little better, and I demonstrate this by receiving the ball and taking it around two players before passing it to a teammate to level the score.

As I give Nev a high-five and get back in position, I know it isn't his fault that he isn't gifted at this sport. He didn't choose to be bad at something. Nobody does. I certainly didn't choose to be bad at Maths, or Science, or any of the other boring subjects that get forced down my throat five days a week. I just don't pick things up as quickly as other people do, just like Nev can't do things with the football like I can. At least he is good in the classroom. His mock exam results were miles better than mine, and he is on course to achieve A's and B's in our end of year exams. I, on the other hand, would consider a C to be a fantastic achievement, but even that is being optimistic.

Mum and Dad think that my poor grades are a consequence of my lax attitude to learning, but it's not quite as simple as that. If all I had to do was sit, listen and revise for the next few months and get an A, then I would do it. But it's not that easy. Things don't seem to stick in my head, or at least not essential things. I can remember the names of all the players in the Aston Villa football team or every score from a dozen games of FIFA on my PlayStation last night, but I can barely remember what I am taught in the classroom each day. Even now, after an hour in Mr Reynold's geography lesson, I've completely forgotten everything he said about those damn tectonic plates. I'm hoping it won't be on the final exam but knowing my luck, it will be.

I receive the ball again, and this time I decide not to pass, opting instead to shoot towards the top corner and go for glory myself. The ball hits the back of the net and I fist-pump the air. That was a great goal. I'm not good enough to be a professional footballer one day, but at least I stand out in this game. I'll stand out when we get back to class too, although that will be for all the wrong reasons.

I hide behind humour and a care-free attitude when I'm in class, not because I'm rude or disrespectful to the teachers but because it's easier than admitting that they are right. They all know the truth, even if my classmates don't. I'm going to fail my exams at the end of the year, and I'm going to leave school with nothing. I might be fine in my life after here or I might not. My teachers worry. My parents worry. Even I worry, although I'd never admit it to anyone.

But maybe I will be okay. Maybe it doesn't matter if I fail all of my exams. Maybe life will find a way of working out for me in the end, just like it did for Mum.

Only time will tell.

5

AMY

I'm back in the school car park again and watching all the pupils pouring out of the building opposite me. I never seem to get a break from this place, even after all these years.

Sharpbell High. It has, is and seemingly always will be a fixture in my life.

I knew I'd be forced to come back here when I decided to buy that house with Nick. We knew this was the closest school, and therefore the most likely one for our children to end up attending. We did briefly consider sending them to Maxwell High but quickly dismissed the idea. That is the only other secondary school in the area, but it has gone downhill a lot over the years by all accounts, whereas my old school has been transformed. Of course, that is more to do with the fire that burnt this place to the ground than it is because of better teaching and budgeting, but you have to take the positives out of that terrible time.

Some people say the fire was the best thing that ever happened to this school because it was getting worse by the year and needed a fresh start, but they don't really mean it. Nobody can seriously believe that what happened here was for the best. I sure as hell don't. I can still remember standing on this playground with all the other pupils and parents the morning after the fire and looking at the charred remains of the school. There was nothing positive about that. I'm sure Michael has fantasised about seeing his school burnt to the ground on occasion, just like I used to do myself. But imagining it is one thing. Actually seeing it before your eyes is another altogether.

Through the sea of pupils heading for the gates, I catch a glimpse of a familiar face from my childhood. It's Mr Montgomery, my old History teacher, although he certainly looks a lot different than he did back when I was in his class. He used to be a tall and handsome man, but age and a lifetime of teaching unruly pupils has taken its toll on him. Now his shoulders are stooped, and the dark mop of hair has gone from his head. He must be ready to retire any day now, but maybe he doesn't want to. Maybe he likes the familiarity of his job. He has worked here for most of his life, after all.

He was one of the few teachers to come back when the school reopened, resisting the pull of employment elsewhere and taking up his old role when the new classrooms were built to replace the burnt ones. He has taught Michael during his time here, and I expect he will teach Bella at some point too. It was strange to sit opposite him at Michael's parents' evening and listen to him commenting on my son's schoolwork when he used to comment on my own. He seemed happy to see me and said that he remembered me, but I don't know if he was telling the truth or just being polite. He must have taught so many people over the years here that I doubt he can remember them all.

I can't understand how anybody would want to spend their entire life within the confines of a school. Being a pupil is compulsory, but being a teacher is voluntary. While I admire and respect the profession now that I am older, I would never dream of being a teacher myself. Just being here now for the school run is more than enough for me.

The sight of my eldest coming towards me is enough to make me stop thinking about Mr Montgomery. I hope Michael is in a good mood. I hope school wasn't the tortured experience today that it usually is for him.

'How was your day, love?' I ask my son as he climbs onto the backseat and pulls his door shut.

'Fine,' he mumbles back, and his head is already buried in his mobile phone, which tells me that I'm not going to get any more conversation out of him until we get home.

Fortunately, any awkward silence between us is cut short by the arrival of Bella, who arrives in the car like the little whirlwind that she is.

'Hi!' she says, slamming the door shut behind her and dropping her heavy rucksack into the footwell. Her bag is full of schoolbooks and homework, whereas I'm not even sure where Michael's bag is these days.

'Good day?' I ask as I reverse out of the parking spot and prepare for round two of trying to avoid running over a mother or child.

'Yeah, I got an A on my French test last week, and Mrs Moss said that I'm definitely going to be in the top set next year!'

I smile as I drive us out of the car park and through the gates, proud of my daughter and her accomplishments. But then I catch a glimpse of my son on the back seat and see that he isn't smiling.

'Did you hear anything more about your coursework?' I ask Michael, referring to the English essay that I know he is due to hear back about soon.

'No,' comes the curt response, and I decide to leave it at that. He's obviously had another bad day at school and just wants to forget about it. I grimace as I drive because I know that isn't an option. As soon as we get home, we are going to sit down and talk about it. It won't be fun, and it won't lead to him enjoying his situation anymore, but it has to be done.

Nick and I have decided it. We are going to hire a tutor, and Michael is going to give these exams his best shot, whether he wants to or not.

THE SECOND LESSON

The clean-up operation after the fire was a big task, and the workers toiled while members of the public gathered and watched. It rained that day, although the relief of water came much too late for the charred remains of what was once Sharpbell High.

Teens gossiped and laughed while others seemed shocked that the place they had spent so much time in had been wiped off the map. Adults stood amongst them, some urging their children to grow up, while others stood in stunned silence, seemingly unbelieving that such a thing could happen in a quiet place like this.

For those tasked with sorting through the rubble and determining the cause of the fire, the audience, just like the rain, was unwelcome.

But then things got even more grim.

Amongst the discovery of burnt tables and chairs, papers from textbooks and even a poster for an upcoming performance of Macbeth, there was something else that had survived the hottest part of the inferno.

Bones.

The second lesson is don't play with fire.

6

MICHAEL

What the hell do my mum and dad want from me now? I've been at school all day, and I just want to unwind and play FIFA in my bedroom, yet they are calling me down to the kitchen. I haven't had any more detentions recently so they can't be mad at me for that. Maybe it is something to do with the chores. I haven't taken the rubbish out again. That's probably what it is.

It's hardly a big deal. I shouldn't have to do it anyway. I'm out all day grinding my way through tedious lessons while they get to stay at home. Dad likes to pretend he is working hard in that study, but I bet he's surfing the web half the time. And Mum only works part-time, so she's not exactly rushed off her feet. Sorry for not taking a minute out of my busy day to take the bin bag out but how about the people who use the bin the most take it out instead?

I'm just about to say that as I walk into the kitchen when I see my parents sitting at the table. That's when I know that this won't just be about some menial household chore. They both look serious, and while they do like to try and instil in me the importance of pulling my weight around the house, surely that doesn't warrant the expressions on their faces right now.

Something else is on their mind. But what is it?

'What's up?' I ask when neither of them speak.

'Can you sit down a minute?' Dad asks, and I can tell that he is trying to make out that this is no big deal because of the way he tries to make it sound, but he's a terrible actor. I can tell when he is nervous because he keeps looking at Mum.

He is looking at her right now.

'What have I done wrong this time?' I ask as I slump into a chair at the opposite end of the table from them.

'Nothing love. You haven't done anything wrong,' Mum begins, and that sounds promising. 'Your father and I have been talking, and we have come to a decision regarding your education.'

'My education?' I repeat back, unsure where this is going. Maybe it would have been better if this had been about chores again. That word doesn't fill me with as much dread as the word education does; that's for sure.

'Yes, your mother and I think that hiring a tutor to help you through these next few months before your exams might be a good idea,' Dad says, but I'm shaking my head before he has even finished the sentence.

'You and Mum think it's a good idea, do you?' I reply, my voice already rising. 'What about asking me? Surely I'm the one who should have the biggest say in that?'

Dad looks at Mum again, and it's clear that he is hoping she will take over from here. I love my old man, but he has spent so much time holed away in his study that he seems to have lost his edge when it comes to social communication. That's why I wouldn't want to work from home, even if I had the chance to one day.

'I know that you aren't keen on the idea,' Mum says, and I stop her there.

'Of course I'm not keen! I spend all day stuck in lessons with teachers that I can't stand. Why would I want to come home and have my evenings spoilt too?'

'It wouldn't be every evening. Once or twice a week. And only a couple of hours at a time,' Mum says like that is supposed to sound appealing to me.

'What's the point? It's a waste of money, and if I haven't learnt this stuff now then I'm never going to!'

I feel a rage burning up from inside myself that takes me a little off guard, and I stop speaking before I can blurt out anymore.

'There is still plenty of time before your exams, love,' Mum says. 'I know you don't care about your GCSE's but you will regret it one day if you don't try your best now.'

'But you didn't try your best and you're okay,' I reply, returning to a defence tactic that has sometimes worked for me in the past.

'I know that I didn't get good grades and I wish I could change that. But there were other circumstances.'

'You mean the fire?'

I know Sharpbell High burnt down during Mum and Dad's last year there and they had to take their exams at Maxwell High instead. I also know that they don't like talking about it. Not many people do from those days. But old newspaper articles about it have been republished online so everyone at school now knows what happened, and I know plenty of people in my classes who wish the school would burn down again.

'Not just the fire,' Mum says. 'But you're right, I didn't apply myself as I could have. But you have the opportunities that I never had. My parents couldn't afford to get me a tutor. If they could have done, then I'm sure that they would have. Instead, I had to sit in those exams and struggle, and I don't want you to go through that.'

'Why do you care so much?'

'We're your parents. We want you to do well,' Dad replies, and I think how that was good of him to field the easiest question of the night.

'But none of my other friends have got tutors!' I protest, which is true although I have the feeling that I know what the answer to that is going to be too.

'Yes I know, love, but none of your friends got E's on their mock exams,' Mum tells me and the word 'E' is enough to shut me up for a minute.

I'm still scarred from the sixty-minute Maths mock exam that I endured a few months ago, which was one of several designed to prepare me for the real thing at the end of the school year. All the exams were hard, but that particular one was on another level. My head was hurting so much when I came out that it almost felt worse than the time I fell over in the playground and got a concussion.

'A's. B's. E's. Who cares? They're just letters. They don't mean anything! You know that I don't want to go to sixth form or uni after this. And I don't want to be a doctor or anything either! So why does it matter what grades I get?'

'It matters to us, love. And it should matter to you. You're smart. We know it, and you know it. You just need a little extra help bringing it out,' Mum says.

'And just because you don't want to go onto higher education right now, that doesn't mean that you won't want to in the future. Lots of people go on to further studies later in life these days. But you won't have that option if you fail your GCSE's.'

That last comment was Dad's input, and I can't say that I'm surprised. I know he is disappointed that I have shown no interest in going to sixth form. He went to college and studied I.T., which sounds boring but he apparently loved it. But I'm not him. I don't want to keep studying. All I want to do is leave education behind and get out into the world to make my own way, whatever that might be. But I've told my parents this a million times and here we are still talking about it.

I hate being sixteen.

'Look, I know you don't want a tutor. How about we have a look around, see if we can find anybody that you might like, just for an hour a week to start with, and we can take it from there?'

Mum's suggestion is supposed to sound appealing, but it just sounds like them getting their way and me suffering even more. But I'm too tired to argue. I just want to get back upstairs and back on the PlayStation. I don't even care anymore.

'Whatever,' I say, getting up from the table and walking out of the room.

My parents don't call me back, which tells me that they are satisfied with how that whole shitshow just went. They think they have won. They think they are going to get me a tutor.

They need to think again.

7

AMY

That went about as well as I expected it to. Michael hates the idea of the tutor, but Nick and I already knew that. The main thing is that he has allowed us to look for one and see how it goes on a trial basis, which is a start. Hopefully, we will find somebody who he can get on with and then we can increase the lessons from there.

One step at a time.

Now that the awkward conversation with our son is over, we can move onto the next step, which is finding somebody to teach our boy. Depending on how this goes, this might be easier or harder than what we have just done.

'There must be a website or something,' Nick says as he passes me the clean cups from the dishwasher to put away.

'I don't just want to hire some randomer off a website,' I reply as I open the cupboard door and place the cups carefully inside. 'I'll speak to the school. There might be somebody that they can recommend.'

'Do you think that's a good idea? It's basically letting them know that we don't think their teachers are good enough and we need to hire our own.'

'They won't see it like that.'

'Are you sure?'

I'm not sure, but what else can I do? I need to find somebody, and I need to find them fast. Michael's exams begin in eight weeks. It might already be too late, but we have to try something. Michael is behaving just like I did when I was heading towards my GCSE's and I know how badly they turned out for me. I need to give him a chance if nothing else.

'Maybe they have some people they can recommend. A company, perhaps?' I say optimistically. It's either that or I'm going to have to take my chances with finding a tutor on the internet, which could be a minefield. But it is the modern way, I suppose. People find love online, as well as all sorts of other things, so maybe that is the best place to find a teacher too.

'I'll do some research,' Nick says as he finishes reloading the dishwasher with the plates from dinner and wipes his hand on a tea towel.

'Thanks love,' I reply, but I'm surprised to see that he means that he is going to do it now. He's heading back towards the study again, but I was rather hoping that we would spend some time together on the sofa.

'You don't have to do it tonight,' I say, hoping he will get the hint and come and sit with me instead of with his laptop again.

'His first exam is in eight weeks. We need somebody sooner rather than later.'

He smiles at me as he heads into the study, then he closes the door behind him. He is back in his happy place again. The peace and quiet of his own private room. That just leaves me to deal with the chaos of the rest of the house.

Perfect.

I head for the stairs, picking up various things that belong to my family as I go. Bella's shoes that have been left lying in the middle of the hallway and her coat which has fallen off the end of the bannister and ended up in a heap on the floor, as well as Michael's trainers, which he changes into when he plays football at lunchtime. He knows he should leave his smelly trainers in the pantry, but he always seems to leave them here instead. Maybe he's forgetful. Or maybe he just doesn't care.

I head up the stairs, wondering what it would be like if I had my own room to escape into like the rest of my family have right now. Nick is in his study, where he says he is researching tutors but he could just be watching football highlights. Michael is in his room where I presume he is playing FIFA and enjoying being away from his parents. And Bella is in her room singing away to whichever pop video she is playing on her iPad, without a care in the world, which is the way it should be for her at least. That just leaves me to wander the empty hallways of the house, picking up after everybody and making sure everything is as it needs to be for the morning when everyone will emerge from their rooms like whirlwinds and expect breakfast to be served.

I love my family, but it is definitely changing. Gone are the days when we would all sit in front of the TV at night and watch something together. Now the kids can't wait to get up to their rooms and close the door, and my husband is the same with his study. If I was less assured in myself, then I might suspect that nobody wanted to spend any time with me, but that's just silly. Children want their own space as they get older, and husbands need it too. I'm the only one here who needs to be around others as much as possible and I know why that is. When I'm with other people, I have less time to reflect.

When I'm alone, I start thinking about the past again.

As I reach the top of the stairs, I think about popping my head into Bella's room and seeing what dance routine she is learning now. I also think about knocking on Michael's door and making sure that he isn't mad at us for bringing up the tutor. But in the end, I head for my bedroom where I will do some tidying up before Nick eventually comes upstairs and joins me for a quick chat before we turn the lights out.

This is family life in suburbia. Nothing much ever happens around here. But that's the way I like it.

The last time something happened around here, the police found a dead body.

8

NICK

I love spending time with my family, but I love being alone too. That's why this study is a godsend. Not only does it give me a place to work during the day, but it offers a place of quiet sanctuary in the evenings whenever I feel like I need a little break from family life. Sometimes I enjoy watching mindless television with Amy, but other times I like to come in here, close the door and watch what I want to watch. Right now, what I want to watch are the highlights from last night's football games. I wouldn't get a chance to watch this outside of here because there would be a million and one other things vying for my attention.

Amy is worried about something. Michael is in a mood again. Bella wants attention. It is usually one of those things that mean my free time evaporates quickly and I'm back to working again before I know it. But not tonight. Tonight, I am going to relax in my study, and no one is going to disturb me.

I'm about five minutes into watching the highlights from the Everton v Chelsea game when I feel a slight pang of guilt. I am supposed to be looking online for a tutor for Michael. That's what I told Amy I was going to be doing in here and it is what I should be doing. But I've been working hard all day fixing tedious server issues for tedious clients and I deserve a little 'me time.' I enjoy the work but it's so intensive that I need my downtime. I'll watch the rest of these highlights before I get back to the more tedious tasks again. I already know the score of this game, and there are three more goals to enjoy yet.

As I recline in my leather office chair that I treated myself to when I made the switch over to working at home full-time, I can't help but be distracted by events outside this quiet and peaceful room. The talk with Michael didn't go well. He doesn't want a tutor, which I understand, because what sixteen-year-old boy would ever want to do more schoolwork? But I know that it is for the best. Michael might think that

GCSE's don't matter, but that's only because he hasn't ventured into the working world yet. He'll soon start to question his lack of effort at school when he finds that all the jobs that he wants to do won't even consider him based on his lack of qualifications.

Exam results aren't everything, but there is no way that I would be able to do the job that I do now without having achieved good grades. To become as qualified as I have in I.T. required me to study at college, and I couldn't have done that without attaining the necessary marks to get there. Work isn't the be-all and end-all of life, but it is a necessary part of it, and we are all going to have to work so we might as well do something that pays well if we can. I'm fortunate to have a well-paid job that allows me to work from home and avoid the grind of the commute and office politics, but I would never be in this position if I hadn't applied myself to my studies when I was younger. I don't want my son to get to my age and regret things. I don't want him to struggle and hate his life like so many other people do when they drag themselves out of bed to go to work in the morning.

I find it impossible to concentrate on the football highlights on my laptop with all of this going on in my head, so I turn them off even though there is still one goal in this match that I haven't seen yet. Heading onto Google, that trusty tool that everybody turns to when they need an answer in their life, I type out the words that I have already typed out several times before after earlier discussions about Michael's impending date with exam disaster.

'How to find a tutor for my son.'

I hit enter and end up with almost 43 million results. I might need to narrow it down a little.

'How to find a tutor in the UK.'

115 million results. It's getting worse. Maybe it would be easier to just teach Michael myself. But I tried that and it didn't go well. We just ended up arguing with each other and he would storm off back to his bedroom. I would get frustrated with him for not understanding something that I thought was quite simple, and he would get frustrated that I have absolutely

no teaching skills and can't see things from his point of view. In the end, I put a stop to the 'lessons' before one of us killed the other. It was a shame because Michael and I get on well the rest of the time. We both enjoy football, and we both like a good action movie. But we aren't compatible when it comes to our views on education. It doesn't help that he is a bad student, and I am a terrible teacher.

I try another search, this time for ***'Tutors in my area.'***

The first option to appear sounds promising. It is a website that claims to be the best site to use to match students with teachers. It makes sense that there would be a site like this online somewhere because there is a site to match people with everything else. Men with women. Women with men. Married women with married men. And that's just relationships. There are sites to help unemployed candidates find jobs, sites to reunite old friends and even sites to connect the living with the dead, which sounds bogus, but my late mum was adamant that the dead could make contact after they have gone.

Funny how we haven't heard from her since she passed.

But right now all I need is this site that will help my son find the right tutor, and it seems that I have very few options. Only two in fact.

A fifty-two-year-old woman called Sue and a twenty-eight-year-old woman called Petra.

Investigating the younger woman's profile first, I see a photo of an attractive blonde woman with a bio that informs me she is from Stockholm and has been tutoring secondary-school age pupils for the last six years. Her background seems to be perfect, and her fees aren't high either. What's more, she only lives on the other side of town so wouldn't have far to come. It seems perfect, and I'm almost about to hit the print button and take my findings to my wife when I pause.

Can I really have this as my suggestion? A young, attractive Swedish woman? I'm sure Michael will be interested enough to give it a go, but I'm not sure my wife will. She's going to think that I have just chosen her because I want a cute woman to visit the house several times a week. Maybe this is a bad idea.

I retreat back out of Petra's profile and click on Sue's instead. She isn't as attractive but that's not the point. She is from Coventry but lives in Nuneaton now, which is where we are, and she has over thirty years' experience in education, particularly at the GCSE level.

This is the one I should print. This is the sensible option. This is the option that won't lead to my wife calling me a pervert.

I sigh and hit print.

Sue it is.

9

MICHAEL

Who the hell is Sue, and why is she sitting in our front room?

'Hello dear,' the mysterious woman says to me when I walk in and see her sitting on the sofa. She seems pleasant enough, but I'm not going to allow her to get too comfortable. If this is who my parents think is going to be teaching me for the next two months, then they can think again.

'This is Sue,' Dad says casually as if introducing me to a random woman in our house after I have just got in from school is perfectly normal.

I refuse to take the hint that my parents are giving me about sitting down and instead stay standing in the doorway. If I sit down and listen to whatever they have to say, then they will think that I am going to go along with it, which I'm not. I'm sure Sue is nice, and I'm sure she enjoys teaching, but she is going to have to find someone else to read her textbooks with.

It sure as hell isn't going to be me.

'I understand your GCSE's are coming up,' Sue says, clearly trying to charm me into telling my parents that they should pay this woman whatever fee she is asking for to tutor me. 'It's quite a difficult time. I remember when I was studying for my exams. They were a little different back then of course, but-'

'Sorry, what's this about?' I say, interrupting the woman before she can get further into what is probably a carefully rehearsed spiel.

'Remember we discussed hiring a tutor to help you with your studies?' Mum says, and I can tell she is nervous about me making her look bad in front of this stranger.

'I do. I also remember that I told you I didn't want one,' I reply, shrugging my shoulders and turning to leave. But even I know it isn't going to be that easy.

'If you could just sit down and we can discuss how it's going to work,' Dad says, and I know that he just wants to be back in his study and out of this awkward situation. But all of this could be over if only they would listen to me and respect my wishes.

I turn back to face the room and take in the ridiculous sight of my parents sitting opposite this random woman. I notice that they have already made her a cup of tea. They didn't offer to make me one. Sue already has her feet under the table. But this is as far as she is going to get.

'Sorry to waste your time Sue but there's been a mistake. I don't need a tutor, and I don't want one either, so you're better off going somewhere that does.'

Sue seems a little surprised by my honesty, and she nervously picks up her tea and takes a sip. I feel bad that my parents have wasted her time, but I don't feel bad for speaking my mind. There must be dozens of people out there who want her to teach them. She should be with them, not me.

'Michael, if you would just sit down. Sue has made an effort to be here, and it would be nice if you listened to what she has to say.'

Mum is trying to manage the situation, but she isn't doing a good job of it.

'It would be nice if you listened to what I have to say too,' I fire back.

She set that one up for me nicely.

'Two hours a week, starting today. Just give it a try,' Dad says, but he only wants me to agree so that he doesn't have to try and teach me himself anymore. That was a disaster. I don't usually argue with my dad, but we would have killed each other if we had spent any more time with those Maths books at the kitchen table. I'm sure Sue is a better teacher than he is, but that still doesn't mean I want to put myself through her lessons, especially when I have already had a day full of them at school. I just want to go to my room.

'No, I'm not doing it,' I say, turning to leave again, and this time I won't be stopping.

'Michael!' I hear mum call after me, but I'm already heading up the stairs and leaving the awkward situation behind. They are the ones who have wasted Sue's time so they can be the ones who apologise and ask her to leave. They knew I didn't want a tutor so they should never have asked somebody to come here.

Eight weeks and all of this will be over.

Why can't they just leave me alone?

I slam my bedroom door shut and flop onto my bed, picking up the console for my PlayStation and starting another game of FIFA. I know that my parents are going to come in here after Sue has gone and scold me for how I behaved in front of her. But what did they expect? She's a complete stranger. If I can't sit down and learn Maths and Science with my own father, then I'm hardly going to sit down and learn it with a randomer.

I do my best to concentrate on the game on screen, but I'm distracted, and I'm 2-0 down before I know it. It's annoying because I'm usually good at this game, but it's hard to focus on it with all this rubbish going on around me. I can't wait to get out of this house and get my own place. I'll find a job, I'll have my own money, and then I'll be free. No more schoolwork. No more exams. No more arguments with my parents.

And no more talk of strangers coming to teach me things that I don't need to know.

I can't bloody wait.

10

AMY

I could kill my son. How dare he be so rude in front of Sue. I could only apologise as I showed her out, but she had barely had time to finish her cup of tea before Michael had dismissed her and stormed upstairs. I'll be having words with him, but I need to calm down first.

I also need to find another tutor.

'What are we going to do about this?' I say to Nick as he picks up Sue's half-drunk tea and carries it into the kitchen.

'I'll have a word with him,' Nick replies but that's not what I mean, and he knows it.

'How are we going to help him with his exams if he won't even give us a chance?' I say, and I feel so frustrated that I could hit something. In the end, I just pick up a tea towel and wipe down the kitchen counter furiously. Cleaning will calm me down, and there's always something to be cleaned around here.

'We could just ground him,' Nick suggests but I don't want to do that. Michael needs to want to sit down and learn, not just do it because he is forced into it. He'll never learn anything that way, and he'll resent us and the whole concept of education even more. We need to find a way of making it more appealing to him.

'Was there anybody else on that website?' I ask as I continue to scrub the counter to within an inch of its life.

'There was another option,' Nick says, popping two slices of toast into the toaster and getting crumbs all over the surface that I just cleaned.

'Why didn't you say so?'

'I wasn't sure if she was suitable?'

'What do you mean?'

'Well, she is much younger than Sue. And...'

'And what?'

I stop cleaning and look at my husband, wondering why he is suddenly being coy.

'Well, she's quite...'

'Quite what?'

'Erm...'

'Expensive? Strict? Strange? What?' I ask, but Nick shakes his head.

'Attractive,' he finally says.

'Attractive?'

'Well not attractive as such,' he quickly replies, backtracking while pretending to fiddle with the dials on the toaster.

'You just said attractive,' I say, becoming more and more amused at how uncomfortable my husband is.

'She's just very different from Sue, that's all.'

'Why didn't you mention her before?' I ask although I think I already know the answer to that one.

'I wasn't sure you would think that she was suitable to teach our son.'

'It sounds like it isn't my son who I should be worried about.'

Nick laughs, more out of nerves than anything else, but I'm glad that something has broken the tension in this house ever since Michael was rude in front of Sue.

'Why don't you show me and I'll decide,' I say, willing to give this other tutor a try if she can get my son to sit still and learn for a moment. It can't go much worse than it just did.

'I'll print off her profile,' Nick replies as his toast pops up. 'But only because she has relevant experience.'

'Of course,' I say, frowning at my husband's lame attempts to downplay this woman's profile picture. I can't wait to see it and see why my husband is so flustered. She must be some kind of goddess to have him all worked up like this. I'm not thrilled by that thought, but maybe that's what we need. Maybe that is the only way we will get Michael to go for this whole tutor thing.

'Try not to get too excited in there,' I call to my husband as he carries his plate of toast into the study to go and print the profile for me. I'm teasing him and he knows that I'm joking.

If only we had left it there.

Little did we know it at the time, but that was the moment when everything would change in our family.

THE THIRD LESSON

The funeral took place two weeks after the fire.

It seemed like half the town came out to pay their respects and maybe they did. Everybody from the school was there in one way or another. Pupils lined the road outside the burnt-out shell of the school as the hearse moved past them. Many of them might not have wanted to be there, but the Headmaster made it mandatory. Teachers stood amongst them, some weeping, others more focused on trying to get some of the unruly members of the crowd to behave. Many of the pupils' parents were there too, paying their respects while thankful that it hadn't been their family that had been destroyed.

That unfortunate family was sitting in the black car that passed the sea of faces. It trundled along past the site of the fire on its way to the church where the service would take place. Inside the car, a grieving woman dabbed at her eyes with a tissue and tried to appreciate the turnout while wishing that none of this was happening.

When the cars had passed, the crowd began to disperse. The details for the temporary school were still being finalised, as were the plans to relocate the end of year exams to Maxwell High and for now, the pupils were free to go home. Some of them were happy about this, unshackled from the burden of lessons and homework and free to do as they wished in the middle of the day. Others seemed more thoughtful and took time to look at the site where the school used to stand, as well as watching the portable cabins being put into place by cranes and trucks. Those cabins would become the school for now, until a more permanent one was built in its place.

But that would take time and time seemed to be standing still today. A funeral always makes people aware of their mortality and everybody who watched the hearse go by felt it, even if they covered it up with laughter, jokes and childish games. Nobody likes to acknowledge the seriousness of the situation. Nobody wants to be reminded that it will be them in that wooden box one day.

The third lesson is that death can come for us when we least expect it.

11

AMY

My husband said this woman was attractive, but he was lying.

She's not attractive.

She's hotter than a goddamn volcano.

Petra is sitting opposite us on our sofa, looking all prim and proper, but I'm trying not to let her appearance affect my decision-making ability. She has the qualifications for this job. She has the experience. She is charging a fair price. And she is very pleasant.

Now we just need to make sure that she gets Michael's approval.

'Can you go and get him?' I ask my husband after my son has failed to appear despite us calling him a moment ago.

'No probs,' Nick says, bounding up off his seat on the sofa and heading to the door quickly. He never moves this fast, and he never says 'No probs.' Maybe he is trying to seem youthful and trendier in front of this woman. Or maybe I'm already reading far too much into things.

'So how many other students are you teaching at the moment?' I ask Petra to fill what would otherwise be an awkward silence.

'Two. Both girls. They are in their last year of school as well,' the woman replies in her Scandinavian accent that sounds a lot more poetic than my Brummie one.

'Have you had a male student before?' I ask. It's the first question that popped into my head, mainly because I want to know if she isn't teaching any at the moment because there have been no offers or because the last one she taught ended up falling in love with her and she had to end the arrangement.

'Of course. I love teaching men. I find that they are better students than women.'

I smile, even though I find it strange to hear her refer to teenagers as men. Michael is certainly not a man, even if he thinks he is. He is still a long way off being grown up. The fact that he still spends all of his free time playing video games is enough to tell me that.

I can hear my husband and son coming down the stairs, so I decide not to ask another question right now. There will be plenty of time for more of them later, but first, we need to find the answer to the only question that matters.

Is Michael going to agree with the idea of having this woman as his tutor?

I'm intrigued to witness my son's reaction when he sees the next option that we have brought for him. I'm expecting him to be a little more receptive to Petra than he was to Sue but maybe not for the right reasons. I know Michael will be attracted to her, just like I know that Nick is too, even though he pretends that he isn't. That might mean my son is willing to give her a chance, but it doesn't mean that they will be compatible as student and teacher. But right now, I need him to agree to this whole thing and not storm back upstairs like he did last time. If he says yes to Petra, then I don't care that it might only be because he fancies her. If it gets him to sit down and do some revising, then that is the main thing. Lord knows nothing else has worked so far.

I watch the doorway as I hear Nick and Michael approaching. It is my husband who walks in first, and he purposefully makes sure he doesn't look at Petra as he walks in because he knows that I am watching him like a hawk. But Michael has no idea what is waiting for him, and that becomes clear when he walks through the door and sees the woman sitting opposite me.

'Oh, hi,' he says quickly, instinctively standing up straighter and pushing his chest out to make himself look bigger and more grown-up than he is.

'You must be Michael,' Petra says, and she stands up and offers her hand to him.

Michael glances in my direction before he shakes it, nervous about being in the presence of a woman like this and even more so because he knows his mum and dad are watching him.

He shakes Petra's hand and looks down at his feet, which I find endearing because he is obviously shy. But the tutor shows no such signs of nervousness. She simply compliments my son on his height and his t-shirt, which displays the logo of one of his favourite bands.

I'm about to stand up and draw the line if she touches one of his arms and asks him if he works out, but she doesn't do and instead sits back down on the sofa and smiles at me.

'This is Petra, and she is from Sweden,' Nick says, holding out his hand towards the woman as if my son needs it pointing out to him who he is referring to, which he doesn't. There's only one Nordic beauty in this room and it sure as hell isn't me. But Nick points her out all the same and I assume it is just another nervous body movement because he is in the presence of such beauty. But I'm not sure why he had to highlight the fact that she is Swedish? Would he have bothered to mention where she was from if she was from Stoke?

I don't know why, but some men seem to have a fascination with Scandinavian women, and my husband is obviously no different. Maybe this was a bad idea. Maybe I should give Sue another call and see if she is willing to give it another try.

But Petra is here now, and Michael is still standing in the room, which means this is already going better than it went with the older woman a couple of days ago. But now that the introductions are out of the way, it's time to get down to why we are all here.

'Can you sit down a minute,' I say to Michael, and I mean for him to take the empty seat beside me, but Petra is already moving up on her sofa and making space for him.

Michael looks at the cushioned seat beside the Swede before sitting down on the floor instead. He obviously doesn't want to sit next to me because he wants to appear grown-up, but he's too shy to sit beside Petra. That might be okay for now but will pose a problem when it comes time for the two of them to revise together.

'Petra is a private tutor and specialises in teaching people for their GCSE exams,' I say, getting to the point. 'We've told her that you are looking for a little help with your Maths.'

Michael shrugs. 'Just a little bit,' he says, and he is clearly trying to make it seem unimportant, but for me it is monumental. It is the first time I have ever heard my son acknowledge the fact that he might need help with certain subjects.

'It just so happens that Maths is my strong suit,' Petra says, flashing a set of perfectly white teeth as she smiles at my son. 'I can teach all subjects, even English if required, but I have most of my experience in Maths. I find that it's the one that students tend to struggle with the most.'

'Because it's the most boring one,' Michael says, obviously trying to be funny in front of our guest. Petra laughs a little, which I know will make my son feel good, but she also keeps her professional nature in front of us.

'I wouldn't call it boring, but it certainly isn't as interesting as some of the other, more creative subjects,' she says.

'How long have you been over here?' Nick suddenly asks, and I'm not sure why that is relevant.

'Four years,' Petra replies.

'Awesome,' Nick says, and I have never heard him use that word either.

Is this what it is going to be like around here if Petra ends up getting the job? Will my husband and son be reduced to two awkward, uncomfortable people who can't sit still, say unnatural words and generally look as if they can't relax until they are alone again?

Maybe this is a bad idea. But then Michael asks her another question, and despite what I suspect his true motivation to be, he is at least still in the room. If this goes well over the next few minutes, then I don't see any reason not to offer Petra the job, at least on a trial basis.

Michael likes her. Nick likes her. And I like her too. Bella hasn't met her yet, but I'm sure she will be excited to have another female in the house. She will probably want to find out how Petra gets her hair looking so amazing. I wouldn't mind finding out too.

By the time the Swedish tutor leaves our home thirty minutes later, I have given her the job.

12

MICHAEL

I never thought I'd say this, but I can't wait to do some revision. Tonight is going to be my first lesson with the tutor that Mum and Dad have found for me, and I can't wait.

Her name is Petra, and she is *gorgeous*.

She should be here in half an hour, so that gives me just a little more time to get myself ready for her arrival. I've already showered and put on a fresh pair of jeans, as well as the same t-shirt that I wore when I first met the Swedish tutor. She told me that she liked it, so I've decided to wear it again. I've also spent time making sure my hair is gelled to perfection and that any spots on my face have been covered up with some of Mum's makeup that she doesn't know I use. I'm looking sharp, and I'm ready to impress Petra.

But there's still time to do more.

Dropping to the floor, I do ten push-ups in a bid to get the blood pumping in my arms so that they will look more prominent when she gets here. I'm not skinny, but I'm not muscular either, although I might start working out more now that I have somebody to impress. The girls at school don't look anything like Petra. They're all plain and boring. But my tutor is stunning.

Maybe there is a chance that something could happen between us. It's highly unlikely, but what have I got to lose? Mum and Dad want me to sit with a tutor twice a week and I have agreed to it. So what if it's only because I'm attracted to that tutor. I only have to pretend that I'm learning. What matters is that I get to spend four hours a week with her.

I've already told my mates about Petra, and they are all jealous, although I haven't been able to show them a photo of her yet. I don't know her surname so I can't find her on social media, but I'm determined to find out tonight. As soon as I have her full name then I can find her profile page online and send it to all of my mates, and then they really will be jealous. I bet some of them will even try and persuade their parents that they need a tutor too. But it won't work because they are all cleverer than me.

The jokes on them.

I'm just about to start my second set of press-ups when I stop suddenly. I shouldn't be exercising. I just showered. What if I end up sweating and Petra thinks I'm smelly? Then she won't let me get closer to her. She might even cancel the lesson and leave. Then Mum and Dad will get that other woman back, and I'll be stuck learning Maths with her instead of with a beautiful Swedish woman.

I get back to my feet and rush towards my bedroom window, opening it wider in an attempt to get more cool air inside and lower my body temperature before I start sweating. It was a good idea to try and get a pump going in my arms, but I need to plan it better. I will do the push-ups before my shower next time. That way, I will look buff and smell good when Petra arrives to teach me.

Checking the time, I see that our first lesson is due to begin in five minutes. That gives me just enough time to review my hair in the mirror again and put another squirt of deodorant on. I'm annoyed because I have run out of aftershave so I can't use any of that tonight. I stupidly wasted a lot of it on some of the house parties that I have been to recently, vainly trying to impress some of the girls from school who were in attendance. But I should have saved it for tonight when I will be in the presence of a real woman. The girls at school wouldn't appreciate good aftershave, but I bet Petra would. Plus it would make me seem older, and that is what I need to do. I'm aware that she is much older than me. I don't know how old exactly, but there must be at least ten years between us. I don't consider it a problem, but she might. That means that I have to make sure that I behave older than my age. I can't be childish around her. I can't talk about playing video games all the time, even though that's all I do. And I can't let Mum and Dad boss me around in front of her. I need them to treat me like an adult when she is here and not their child.

I have already had this discussion with them, although I had to do it in a way that wouldn't reveal the fact that I have a massive crush on my tutor. I just told them that they aren't to come in when we are in a lesson, nor are they to embarrass me with any stories about what I was like as a child. I need Petra to see me as a grown man, which I'm not quite but will be soon. If she does, then I have a chance with her.

That is all I can ask for.

I just wish I had some damn aftershave left. Then I have an idea. I might not have any aftershave, but I bet Dad does. It will be in his toiletries bag in the bathroom.

I leave my room and reach the door at the end of the hallway.

But it's locked.

'I need to get in,' I say to whoever is on the other side of it.

'Go away,' I hear my annoying little sister shout back.

'Bella, stop hogging the bathroom!' I call back.

Then I hear a knock at the front door.

It's too late.

The tutor is here.

13

NICK

The tutor is here. But I better let Amy answer the door. I don't want it to look like I am too excited to get a glimpse of the sexy woman that has just turned up at our house. I'll play it safe and stay in my study. I'll let my wife welcome Petra in, and then I'll leave my son to his lesson. There's no need for me to go out and say hello, even if it would be titillating to have a little chat with the tutor. But I'm a grown man. I'm married. It's silly to feel all giddy about the presence of an attractive woman who isn't my wife. It's not as if I want to do anything. I love Amy. I'm happy. But I spend all day in this house, and I haven't flirted with another woman in years. It doesn't have to mean anything. It would just be nice to do - a little confidence booster. Getting a smile off Petra would give me a warm glow, then I can come back to my study and get on with my night.

God, I need to get out more.

I hear my wife greeting the tutor, and then I hear her calling upstairs to our son. He will hate that. He has expressively told us that we are not to treat him like a child in front of Petra, nor are we to do anything that might embarrass him. He hasn't said why, but it is obvious.

He fancies her.

That's my boy.

If I'm honest, I'm just glad that we have found a way of getting Michael to sit down and do some extra studying. I don't care if he is smitten with his tutor, nor do I care if he spends half of the lessons fantasising about what it would be like to be intimate with her. As long as he spends at least some of the lesson learning things that are going to help him pass his exams in eight weeks, then that is all that matters.

Petra will be coming here twice a week, on Tuesdays and Thursday evenings, for two hours at a time. I am hoping that the extra work she does with my son will give him the boost he needs ahead of the tests that are going to carry him into his adult life. But part of me feels a little sad that we left it so late before finding him a tutor, although that's not just because I wish my son had more time to learn.

It's because I wish there would be more visits from the pretty Swede.

I shake my head and tell myself to stop being daft. I'm forty. It's fine for Michael to have a crush on another woman, but it's silly for me. I'm far too old for all that malarky. I wouldn't even know what to do with a woman like Petra even if I had the chance, which I never will because I don't want to have it.

Think about Amy, I tell myself, and it seems to be working right up until the moment when I hear the Swedish accent on the other side of my study door.

God, it's sexy.

It sounds like Amy is showing Petra through to the kitchen where the lesson will be held with Michael. They are going to sit at the table, and we are not going to interrupt them. Amy did float the idea of having them use my study to conduct the sessions, but I managed to talk her out of that, telling her that it would be a big job to tidy all my paperwork up and that there is actually more space at the kitchen table than there is at this desk. In reality, it is because I don't want to give up my study because that would mean that I have nowhere that I can retreat to whenever I feel like I need some space. If Michael and Petra are in here, then I'll either be stuck on the sofa with my wife watching some awful reality show or I will be sat in Bella's bedroom having my hair braided again. I love my daughter to bits, but I don't have much hair left now, and I'll have even less if I allow her to keep tying it into tight bobbles.

There is another reason though why I didn't want Michael's lessons to be held in here. I don't like the thought of Petra sitting in this seat and touching my things. It's not because she might damage anything or misplace something. It just makes me feel excited that she could be sitting where I am right now, and I need to prevent anything that will make me feel even more thrilled about her than I already do.

A distraction, that's what I need. I reach for my headphones and stuff them into my ears before I can be seduced anymore by the dulcet tones of the Swedish voice outside. Like the sailors who were pulled onto the rocks by the songs from the Sirens in Greek mythology, I need to block my hearing so I can't be seduced into doing something that will not end well for me.

As I begin to play some more football highlights on my laptop and listen to the sound of the commentator through the earplugs, I feel good about how mature I am being. Eight weeks and Petra will be gone, and then Amy will be the only woman I see and hear around here. My wife will remain while the pretty Swede will be just a pleasant memory.

I can do it. It's easy. Just don't think about her and how perfect she looks.

But what about my son? He has to sit with her and try to study Maths.

Good luck, my boy.

You're going to need it.

14

MICHAEL

I haven't listened to a word of what my tutor has said to me since I sat down. It's not that I don't like the sound of her voice. I do. *It's lovely*. It's just that her beauty is overwhelming.

I can't believe education can be so fun. If only all my teachers had been like Petra, maybe I wouldn't be in this position now. But I'm glad I am. I'm glad I get to spend some time with this majestic woman.

'Michael?'

I snap out of my daydream when I realise that Petra is staring at me. I quickly look down at the textbook in front of me and frown to make it look like I'm searching for an answer. But I have no idea what the question is, so I've got no chance of finding it.

'I was asking if there is any particular area you would like to start with first? An area that you feel needs improving the most?'

I keep my eyes on the book on the table because looking up will distract me even more. Petra wants to know if there is a particular part of Mathematics that I struggle with. Where do I start? It would be easier to say all of it. But then I might come across as being stupid, and I don't want to do that, although maybe she wouldn't care. She is here to help me, after all. Maybe I should just be honest.

'I've always struggled with probabilities.'

Petra nods and makes a note on a piece of paper. Her handwriting is small and neat, not at all like mine. My English teacher once said that my writing resembled a drunk spider that had staggered across the page. I thought that was quite funny and the rest of the class did too, but my parents didn't. They accused me of being lazy and said I knew perfectly well how to write, but I just couldn't be bothered. They are right, of course. I can't be bothered. I'm not going to be a writer when I leave school, so why does it matter if my handwriting is sloppy? Then again, I'm not going to be a mathematician either.

What am I going to be?

'Anything else?'

I turn a few pages in the GCSE Maths book that Petra brought with her, scanning my eyes over all the various topics of this subject that I hate so much.

Algebra. Geometry. Fractions.

It's all so dull and all so painful. I've spent years of my life listening to people talk about these things, and hardly any of it has stuck in my brain. It's hardly a surprise when it's so boring. I'm not sure how Petra is going to make any of this more appealing to me. But who cares? As long I get to sit with her, that's alright with me.

'Michael?'

'Oh, sorry.' I'm aware that I have slipped into a daydream again. I need to stop doing that, or she is going to think that I'm weird.

'I've never been a fan of Pythagoras,' I say when my eyes land on that dreaded word on Page 47 in this chunky textbook.

'Who is?' Petra replies, and I look up to see her smiling at me. I watch her write down that word and even from across the table, I can read it so clearly. She really is a neat writer. That is when I realise that this woman is the complete opposite of me. She is clearly someone who has dedicated herself to learning. She writes well and speaks well, even in her second language. She obviously knows everything about what is in this textbook, or she wouldn't be preparing to teach it. Maybe I shouldn't have been so quick to dismiss further education. Maybe college and university would be good.

Maybe those places are full of people like her.

'Okay, I've already made a little plan of how we should tackle these next eight weeks before your exam,' Petra says, and she slides a piece of paper across the table towards me. 'I will adjust it based on areas you think need more work, as well as what I observe over our first few lessons. But take a look and let me know what you think.'

I missed half of what she just said because I was too busy noticing how perfect her hand was when she passed me the piece of paper. But I tell myself to focus and read the writing on it now so that I can give her a proper answer and not just some mumbled form of agreement.

'This looks good,' I say, even though it is just a schedule of revision for the next eight weeks that promises to be very difficult, very laborious and in the end, probably pointless.

'I will share a copy with your parents as well. But I just wanted to let you have a look first and see what you thought.'

I wince a little at hearing Petra mention my parents as if they need to supervise and double-check everything that involves me. It makes sense that they do because they are paying this woman and want to make sure that they are getting value for money. But it is a reminder to me of how young I am and how much older Petra is. I wish we had met somewhere else and not in my mum and dad's house. Somewhere for adults, like a bar or club. Then she could see that I'm not some child who needs supervising. I can be a grown-up.

I can be someone she might be interested in.

'Is that okay?' Petra asks, and I silently curse myself for not answering her quicker again. She must be starting to wonder what she has got herself into now considering all my long pauses and lack of speech. I don't want her to think I'm stupid. I want her to think that I'm cool.

'Yeah, this looks alright,' I say, shrugging my shoulders and trying to give off a carefree vibe that will tell her how chilled and relaxed I am about this and life in general. But she doesn't seem to warm to my display of casualness and takes back the piece of paper without a smile, which upsets me a little.

'Okay, if you turn to page eighteen and we'll get started with probability.'

She's very professional. I wish she would just stop talking about Maths and start talking about herself. Her background. Her experiences. Her hopes. Her dreams.

Her surname.

I still need that so I can find her on social media later. But there's time. For now, I do as I am told. I turn to page eighteen and prepare to be taught probability.

What's the probability that Petra and I might share a kiss at some point over the next eight weeks? I feel bad when I predict that the probability is most likely zero.

But I didn't know then that I was going to learn a lot over the next eight weeks and my predictions on everything would change.

Including that one.

15

AMY

For the first time in a while, I feel completely at ease. My son's looming exams have caused much worry about the future, but those worries have been eased by our hiring of a tutor. Petra is in the kitchen with Michael right now helping him with those parts of Maths that he struggles with the most. I'm not expecting miracles, but I feel confident that she will help him to perform better when the big day comes at the end of the term.

We have told her to focus on Maths because that is Michael's weakest subject, but depending on how it goes, we might be able to get some Science in too. Petra has told us that she is an all-rounder so we might as well use her talents while we have her. She isn't too expensive either, although I'm going to have to make a few cutbacks in the short term while we are paying her. I'll pick up a few cheaper options in the supermarket during the weekly shop, and I'll skip having my nails done for the next couple of months too. Buying nicer food and having a manicure every now and again are the little luxuries I treat myself to, but I can make a sacrifice for Michael's education. The important thing is that he has the best chance to succeed in his exams and I am confident now that we have given him that.

I'm sitting on the sofa watching Ant and Dec run through one of their typical comedy routines on yet another reality show that they are hosting when I give in to the urge that has been niggling at me for a while. I pick up my mobile and tap on the Facebook app, but I'm not on the hunt for status updates and photos of family and friends.

I'm going to have a little peek at Petra's profile.

I have her full name, so I could have done this sooner, but I didn't want to. I have told myself that it is because I trust her and don't feel the need to go snooping, but it's not really that. It's because I expect to feel more than a tinge of jealousy when I see that she probably looks even better in her online photos than she does in real life. But I can't help myself right now. I want to do some social media snooping.

I type her name into the little search bar and hit the button, and her profile is the one that pops up first. There aren't too many people with the same name as her and of them, she is the only one who has left Scandinavia and changed her address to Nuneaton. Not the typical place for a Swede to end up, but I'm glad she is here. My son would be stuck without her.

Her profile page opens up on my phone, and I was right. She does look even better in her profile photo than she does in real life. I know most people do, but this is ridiculous. She literally looks like a model. The blonde hair. The blue eyes. The pale skin. *And that smile.*

I'm surprised she has ended up being a tutor. With looks like this, she could have been anything that she wanted to be.

I scroll down her timeline, but there isn't much there because she is private, which means I can only see the odd time she has changed her profile photo. I will have to add her as a friend to see more, but I don't want to do that because then she will know that I have been stalking her. Plus then she will see my profile photo and it is not as flattering as hers. Compared to this woman, I look like a yeti that has walked out of the sea. Okay, I'm not that bad, but I can't compare to Petra.

Nobody can.

I hope Michael is concentrating in there. I'm sure he must be finding it difficult. In an ideal world, his tutor wouldn't be somebody who I know he will find attractive but if that is what it takes to get him to revise then so be it. I know he likes women, although he has never brought one home to introduce to me. He makes out like he is shy, but I see him texting on his phone and being all coy, and I know it's not just his friends from the football team that are sending him messages. But he's only sixteen, so I'm glad he hasn't got himself into a serious relationship with one of the girls from his classes yet. He has plenty of growing up to do and plenty of time to fall in love. He certainly doesn't need anything else to distract him from his schoolwork.

Having looked at as much as I can on Petra's profile, I retreat out of it sheepishly, feeling a little bad for looking her up but satisfied that she is at least who she says she is. As soon as I am back on my newsfeed, I see all the posts from my friends, and this is more what I am used to. Middle-aged mums writing statuses asking for recommendations for things that could help them make extra cash or save extra cash. There is also the usual array of photos of glasses of wine, children's drawings and a few book covers, some of which come recommended, some of which are to avoid.

I wonder what Petra's timeline looks like. Much more interesting than mine, I imagine. All bars and nightclubs, or maybe yoga sessions and healthy eating. Young, tanned and toned people living their lives. It's time to come off social media. It always leaves me feeling like I'm missing out on something.

Putting my phone back down, I turn my attention back to Ant and Dec. The two cheeky chappies are up to more antics, and I smile because this is all I need.

My family is safe. I am happy. And I have a glass of red wine.

I don't need to share any of it on Facebook to know that.

THE FOURTH LESSON

The tears hadn't stopped even though the funeral had finished two weeks ago. For the woman who had lost so much, she had to wonder if they ever would. It wasn't easy to move on, least of all because she found herself sitting in a home that was full of the photos of the person she had lost.

That fire hadn't just taken a life. It had taken her soul too.

Sometimes the sky outside the window was clear and blue, and other times it was dull and grey, but the one thing that stayed the same was the feeling in her stomach. It was the feeling that she had lost something that she could never get back.

She noticed the textbooks on the bookcase across the room and wondered if there was one that would teach her how to deal with being a widow. But there wasn't. They were all about Maths, Science and English, and there was even a book on Religious Studies.

But nothing about how to handle grief.

Education had given her husband's life so much meaning and purpose, but it had also ripped it apart. School hadn't been particularly fun for her, but she never hated it as much as she did right now. School was no longer just some tedious part of everybody's life. For her, it was the place that had taken the life of the man she loved.

Why had he had to work late that night of all nights? Why hadn't he just come home on time and avoided the devastating fire? Why couldn't he still be here now?

There were no answers to be found, which was why she opened the second bottle of wine. It was also why she reached for the pills. Soon there would be no waking her up and then she would be with her husband in the afterlife.

The fourth lesson is that for some people, the only way to get over death is to enter into it too.

16

MICHAEL

I was right. My mates are jealous of me. That's because I managed to find out what Petra's surname was and now I am showing them all a photo of her on my phone.

It was Svensson. Petra Svensson.

How exotic.

'You jammy sod!' Nev says as he gets a good look at the Facebook photo I have just shown him. 'As if she is your tutor!'

'You better believe it,' I say with a smug grin on my face and it only gets wider as my phone gets passed around the group.

We're sitting in class waiting for our form teacher to come in and start the day, but for now, I am enjoying my five minutes of fame. The lads here think I am some kind of God for having Petra as my personal tutor and I am more than happy to let them keep thinking that.

'How old is she?' asks Jonny, another one of my mates.

'Twenty-eight,' I reply, raising my eyebrows suggestively.

'She's gorgeous,' says Ben, another one of my friends who is just as jealous as the rest of them.

'You should see her in real life. She's even better than the photos,' I say, happy to exaggerate because why not?

'No way! Is she?' Jonny cries, and I nod to confirm that I am telling the truth.

'I can't believe this. I get good grades and get nothing, and you get bad ones and end up with her!' Nev moans and I laugh at my best friend's jealousy.

'Lads, what can I say? Work smarter, not harder.'

We're having so much fun looking at Petra's picture that we fail to notice that our form tutor, Mr Hamilton, has walked in and is now standing at the front of the room with a stern expression on his face. Everybody else is in their seats, but the four of us are still crowded around my phone at the back of the room.

'Is there something that you would like to share with us?' Mr Hamilton asks, and that's when we notice him.

I quickly grab back my phone and head for my seat. 'No, it's alright,' I reply as I slump into my seat and put my mobile in my pocket.

'Michael's got a fit tutor, sir,' Nev says cheekily, and I do my best not to laugh because I know that Mr Hamilton won't be impressed with that comment.

'Excuse me?' our teacher asks, and I shake my head at Nev to tell him to shut up.

'Michael's got a tutor, sir. And she's from Sweden!'

That was Jonny this time, and it seems I made a mistake showing my friends the photo here. I should have waited until we were on the playground at lunchtime. But I couldn't wait. I had to show them as soon as possible.

I had to show them how lucky I was.

'You have a tutor, Michael?' Mr Hamilton asks me, and I can feel the eyes of everybody in the class on me now.

'Err, yeah, I do,' I reply.

'And what is the purpose of this tutor?'

'Just helping out with my exams,' I say, feeling less prideful now and more embarrassed.

I wonder if Mr Hamilton is going to make a big deal about me having a tutor. Maybe he will make a joke and everyone will laugh at me for needing extra help with my studies. Even having a hot tutor isn't worth being made fun of.

'That's very good, Michael. Very industrious. I hope it helps.'

Then he sits down at his desk and opens his folder, and I feel a sense of relief. He isn't mad at me, nor has he made fun of me. He is impressed that I am doing extra-curricular studies. And so he should be. I am a hard worker. A model student. A perfect pupil.

Yeah, right.

I smile at my friends who had been expecting me to get in trouble and lean back in my seat, satisfied with how life has turned out for me over the last couple of days. Okay, so I haven't actually learnt anything since my lessons with Petra started, but that's not the point. It's not her fault that I'm too distracted by her beauty to listen to anything that she is saying to me. But the main thing is that I have the respect, admiration and envy of my friends. And even Mr Hamilton is happy with me, which is something that I thought would never be the case.

I feel so calm and collected that I want to put my feet up on the desk and recline even more, but I better not push my luck. I'm on a winning streak, but there's no need to overdo it. Hopefully, my good fortune will carry onto the playground during the lunchtime football match. But I'm not even that excited about lunchtime right now. I'm more excited about tomorrow night.

I'm more excited about the second lesson with my tutor.

17

AMY

I've noticed the change in my son. It's been impossible not to. He walks a little taller. He answers me with actual words instead of grunts. And he is smiling. I'm pretty sure that I know what the reason is for his newfound positivity, but I'm not complaining. I hired Petra to improve Michael's academic ability, but she has improved his mood as well, and that is a welcome bonus. Instead of having to walk around eggshells with my son in case he erupts and goes storming off to his bedroom, Nick and I feel like we can talk to him about things now and he will actually talk back.

'How was your day, love?' I ask him as he climbs into the backseat of my car and closes his door.

'It was alright,' he replies and getting Michael to say that school was alright is akin to getting a stranger in the street to say that he will give me a million-pound cheque. It has never happened before.

'How was Geography?'

'Yeah, not bad. I got 60% in last week's test.'

'That's better,' I say because it is. I know Michael hates Geography, or rather he hates the person who teaches him Geography. Mr Reynolds is his least favourite teacher, and my son's performances in his lessons reflect that. But it seems that the introduction of a tutor has given Michael a fresh impetus to apply himself. Petra hasn't been teaching him Geography, or at least she shouldn't have been, but it is clear that her introduction into his life has already had a positive effect. Whether that is down to her professional skills or her appearance remains to be seen, but the results are all that matter at this stage. Seven weeks to go to Michael's final exams and all I care about is that he does as well as he can do.

'Come on, Bella. Hurry up!' Michael cries, and I turn to see him looking out of the car window at the school across the playground.

I smile a little because I know why he is in such a rush. He wants to get home and freshen up before Petra arrives at six for his latest lesson. Normally Michael would spend the whole evening in his room playing on his PlayStation and showing no interest in personal hygiene. But based on what he did before his previous lessons with the tutor, I know that he will now be showering, gelling his hair and applying liberal doses of Nick's aftershave.

Oh to be sixteen again. That age when you are so unconfident within yourself that you spend every second trying to make yourself look better to try and catch somebody's attention. I was the same when I was a teen. It's a far cry from where I am now. At forty, I sometimes go days without putting any makeup on and stuffing my dark hair into a bobble is preferable to spending hours straightening or curling it. But that's only because I have already impressed the object of my desire, so I no longer need to put the work in. I caught Nick's eye when we were sixteen, and now he is mine. But the current generation of teens are going through that stage of wondering if anybody will ever like them enough to be in a relationship with them and my son is no different. He wants his sister to hurry up so that he can give himself the best chance at looking good for the pretty woman that is coming to our house.

It's cute. *As long as that is all it is.*

I just hope my son doesn't try and do something that will cause Petra to feel uncomfortable and end the lessons early. But I know Michael isn't like that. He's too shy to actually show her that he likes her. He'll just keep gelling his hair to within an inch of its life and dousing himself in too much aftershave. All innocent and harmless and whatever it takes to get him to sit down and read a damn textbook.

I suddenly spot my daughter walking across the playground towards us. She is chatting animatedly with Lily, her best friend, and it warms my heart to see it. They have been besties since primary school, and I'm glad they are going to be together for their time at secondary school too. Everybody needs a best friend.

'There she is,' I say because I know that Michael will be getting increasingly agitated about how his sister is making him late for the shower.

'About time,' he mutters.

I smile again, and I'm just about to start the engine when I see Neville, Michael's best friend, rushing towards our car.

'Is Neville okay?' I ask as the pimple-faced teen reaches the vehicle.

'He's never okay,' Michael replies sarcastically as he winds down his window.

'Have fun tonight you jammy git,' Neville says as he reaches the open window. 'And say hi to Petra for me!'

Michael laughs before looking at me a little sheepishly.

'Hi Neville,' I say to the panting teenager beside my car.

'Oh, hi Mrs Lever,' he says, and he looks as if he hadn't expected to see me in the car with my son. He quickly rushes away after that.

'So you've told your friends about your tutor then,' I say, raising my eyes at my son through the rear-view mirror.

'I just mentioned that I am having extra lessons,' Michael replies.

'Of course you did,' I say, just as Bella arrives at the car.

'Finally!' Michael cries as his sister takes her seat and closes her door.

'Shut up. We're usually waiting for you,' Bella snaps back, and my daughter is right.

'Go easy on your brother,' I say as I reverse out of the spot. 'He's got a busy night ahead of him.'

'Michael loves Petra!' Bella teases, and I can't help but laugh even though I know I shouldn't encourage my children to wind each other up.

'Shut up! I don't!' Michael fires back, and he looks furious, which only makes Bella keep saying it.

I smile as I drive through the school gates and out of the school car park. I'm going to miss moments like this when Michael leaves school. I'm going to miss having both my children in the car every day.

Little did I know it at the time, but that wasn't all I was going to miss by the time the school year was out.

18

PETRA

I'm trying to concentrate on the task at hand, but it's difficult when I'm being overwhelmed with the fumes coming from my pupil. Michael has obviously put on a lot of aftershave for our lesson tonight, presumably to try and impress me. While I appreciate the fact that he has made an effort to smell nice, I would prefer it if my eyes weren't watering right now. The air is heavy with the smell of his bottled scent, and all I can think is thank God that there are no naked flames in here.

One stroke of a match and I feel like this whole kitchen would go up in flames.

That's not to say that I don't like the aroma. On the right man, this particular fragrance is very desirable. But on a sixteen-year-old boy with half a gallon of hair gel on his head? Not so much.

I recognise the smell of the aftershave from the first time I visited this house. But it wasn't Michael who was wearing it that day. It was his father, Nick. I caught a whiff of the scent when he opened the door for me and welcomed me inside, and I have to say that it made me even more attracted to him than I initially was. Coupled with his height, his handsome looks and his gentlemanly nature, I found myself instantly intrigued by the man of this house.

Of course, he is married to the pleasant and polite Amy, so he is off-limits. Or at least he should be. Stranger things have happened. But for now, I need to concentrate on the task at hand. I need to somehow get Michael to understand what I am trying to explain to him.

'The probability of a seed developing into a plant is given as 0.32. If 1,000 seeds are planted, how many plants would be estimated to grow?'

I allow Michael a moment to study the three options, which are 3, 32 or 320.

The teenager's brow is furrowed, and I can almost hear the cogs turning in his head. He might look cute if it wasn't for the fact that the gel on his head was shining beneath the kitchen spotlights and the volume of aftershave on his body was burning my nostrils.

'Erm, thirty two?' Michael suggests.

'Not quite,' I say. 'Take another look.'

Michael scratches his head and lets out a deep breath before returning his eyes to the page.

I wait patiently, not because we have the time but because I know it won't really make a difference how fast we work. His Maths exams are in seven weeks and based on what I have seen from him in the first couple of lessons, he is not going to be ready in time to pass them. Sure, I can give him a better chance and probably improve him a grade or two, but is it really worth all the time and effort?

Of course, it's worth the effort for Amy and Nick, and maybe it is for Michael too, but what about me? I have many talents in life, but I am wasting them by spending my time doing pointless exercises like this.

'320?' Michael asks after a tedious moment of silence.

'That's correct. 'How did you get there?'

I ask the question even though I know exactly how he got there. He didn't use any real logic or knowledge of the exercise to find the answer. He just guessed. He had a 50/50 chance of getting it right after he had got the first one wrong, and this time he had been lucky. It will be interesting to see if he admits that.

'Erm, well.' Michael begins. 'I just guessed.'

I smile at his honesty as well as make a mental note of it. People would think that it would only be the student who would learn something in this situation, but they would be wrong. The teachers can learn so much too.

'Don't worry about it, you got it right, that's all that matters,' I say, turning the page for him and looking for the next question. 'And it's probability after all. The odds were that you had a good chance of getting it.'

He smiles at me, and I can see that he is pleased that I am pleased. He's probably terrified of looking young and stupid in front of me, but he doesn't have to worry about that. I already know that he is young and stupid, so there isn't much that he can do at this point to change that fact.

I read out another question and allow Michael time to formulate an answer before I find my eyes being drawn to the closed door at the other end of the kitchen. I'm not exactly sure what the room is, but I know that Nick is in there. He came out of the room briefly when I arrived tonight, and he went back in there just before the lesson started. I imagine it is an office or study, but I can't be sure. All I know is that he is in there alone now and I am stuck here teaching his stupid son probability.

What is the probability of me being alone in that room with Nick? What is the probability of me telling him how attractive I find him? What is the probability of me giving him a kiss?

And what is the probability of him kissing me back?

'Forty five!' Michael says, snapping me out of my daydream.

'That's the right answer,' I reply, actually impressed that he managed to get one right first time. I had thought the probability on that would have been particularly low.

'Okay, so I've got a good understanding of where you are at with this,' I tell my student as I close the book and pick up a blank piece of paper nearby. 'Now how about I show you a little trick that will help you in your exam when I'm not there?'

Judging by the grin on Michael's face, he seems eager to know what it could be.

But I already knew that.

The probability was high on that one.

19

AMY

My son's study session has just finished, and I have shown the Swedish tutor to the door. By all accounts, it was a productive lesson. I chatted with Petra for ten minutes after she had completed her lesson with Michael and she told me that things had gone well. I was worried that she might have just been saying that because her student was standing within earshot, so I had waited for him to disappear upstairs before trying to get more confirmation. But Petra said the same thing after he had gone.

Michael is a good student. He clearly struggles with some areas, but it's nothing that can't be improved before the big day. So far, it's going well.

I feel relieved to learn these things, and it has confirmed my belief that Petra was the right person for this job. I also feel slightly guilty for spending so much time thinking about her appearance and not her professional skills. It shouldn't matter what she looks like. The important thing is that she is a good teacher and it seems that is exactly what she is.

We also had a brief chat about other things before she left this evening. She asked me what I did for work, and I told her about my part-time job, although I found myself bigging it up slightly and making it seem a little more impressive than it really is. I'm not exactly sure why I did this, but maybe it has something to do with me not wanting to feel too inferior to a brainy tutor. I have no doubt that she has me beat in the brains department, never mind the looks, but that doesn't mean I can't at least try and make myself look a little better around her. I even put a touch of makeup on before she got here but not enough so that anyone in my family would notice it and be amused by it.

Just enough to cover a few blemishes.

Just enough to make me feel pretty enough to stand next to Petra.

Then she asked me about what Nick does for work, and she seemed interested in the fact that he worked from home. I imagine that is because her job requires her to go to other people's homes on a daily basis, so she is probably envious of somebody who gets to have the work come to them. I was going to suggest to her that she could easily have her students visit her home instead of her going to them, but I didn't want to. I'm glad she comes to us. It's one less car journey to fit into my day. Besides, I don't know her personal circumstances. Her home might not be suitable for holding private lessons. Maybe she lives in a small flat. Maybe she lives with other people. A friend or a boyfriend, perhaps. There's so much I don't know about this woman, but I know what I need to. She is a qualified teacher with good experience. Anything else beyond that is her private life.

I wished Petra a good evening and told her I would see her in a few days for the next lesson and now I am going in search of my husband in his study. I feel like letting him know that the coast is clear now or he might end up staying in there all night. I know he won't be working at this hour. I bet he's watching football highlights on his laptop again.

I open the door without knocking in a bid to catch him out, but he isn't in here. I look around the empty study, but there is no sign of my husband. That's strange. Where else could he be?

'Nick?' I call out as I leave the study and walk across the kitchen. I know he isn't upstairs because I came from there when I heard Petra and Michael finish their lesson. So where the hell is he?

I reach the bottom of the stairs and see Michael coming back down. He has got changed out of his jeans and shirt and is now wearing his favourite jogging bottoms and an old t-shirt that definitely could do with a wash. He obviously feels comfortable wearing these now that Petra has gone.

'Have you seen your dad?' I ask him as he walks down towards me.

But Michael shrugs as he passes me by and heads for the kitchen, presumably to find himself a snack in the fridge.

I decide to go upstairs and check to make sure. Maybe he slipped into the bathroom without me noticing. He must be up there. Where else could he be? The garden? That would be weird. It's gone eight, and it's pitch black outside. I don't know why he would be out there.

'Nick?' I call out when I reach the upstairs landing. But the only thing I hear up here is the sound of music coming from Bella's room. I should go in and tell her to turn it down and start getting ready for bed, but I want to find my husband first. A quick check on the bathroom confirms that it is clear. He isn't up here.

He must be outside.

I go to our bedroom window and look out on the back garden. It's pretty dark, but the light from the kitchen offers enough for me to see the grass and the path leading down to the shed. But there is no sign of any movement out there.

I go into Michael's room, which is risky because he could come back up at any moment and have a go at me for being in there, but I want to get a look out of his window. That's because it offers a view of the front of the house and I'm wondering if Nick is out there.

Stepping around the PlayStation consoles and the empty plates on the floor, I reach the window and pull the curtains aside.

That's when I see my husband. He is standing on the driveway beside his car. But he isn't alone.

He is talking to Petra.

He is smiling. She is laughing.

Then she touches his arm.

And now I want to know what the hell they are talking about.

20

NICK

I close the back door and rub my arms to get a little warmth into them as I head for the study. I had only planned on being outside for a couple of minutes, but then Petra had left the house and I had ended up talking to her on the driveway. I'd gone out to get the manual from my car to help with the online car insurance quote that I'm working on, and I'd gone out the back way to avoid seeing anybody. But then I had closed the car door and turned around to see Petra standing right in front of me.

It's the first time I had properly spoken to her since she came to our house to meet us all before the lessons with Michael began. She seemed happy to see me and asked me how my work was going, which must mean that Amy has told her that I work from home. I told her that everything was going fine but then quickly said I had been busy, so she didn't think that I had been hiding out in the study when I didn't need to be. But she didn't seem to read much into it, unlike Amy, who always wants to know what I'm up to in there at night.

I asked Petra how the lessons with Michael were going and was pleased to hear that they are going well. Of course, I'd already asked my son this before, but he was pretty coy about the whole thing. It's hard to get an in-depth answer from somebody when they are playing a video game and have a mouth full of toast. But Petra had told me that Michael was a good student and that she was confident that she would be able to improve his understanding of his most challenging subject in time for his exams. I was glad to hear that, and I know Amy would be too. It's not just about making sure that we get value for our money from the lessons, it's about making sure our son has more opportunities open to him when he leaves school and decides what he wants to do next.

I had expected the conversation to end there, and I had been positioning myself to head inside when Petra had suddenly asked me what aftershave I was wearing. I had been surprised by the question and hadn't really had a proper answer for her. I'm not actually sure what it's called. Amy got it me for Christmas, and it's French, but that's about the depth of my knowledge on the matter. I can't say I have spent much time reading the bottle. Petra had smiled and told me that it smelt nice, whatever it was, and I have to admit it felt good to get a compliment from a woman like her. It's the first time in years that I have had a compliment from somebody other than my wife, and even those aren't exactly forthcoming on a regular basis.

I had told her that I'm not exactly well educated on male grooming products and made a joke about what I consider to be my rather shabby appearance. It was more to ease my slight awkwardness at receiving the show of interest from Petra in the first place rather than any real attempt to be funny. But Petra had laughed and touched my arm slightly as she dismissed my display of self-deprecation and told me that I looked good for a guy who worked from home and didn't have to make an effort if he didn't want to. That was when I realised that she wasn't just being nice to me.

She was flirting with me.

That was also when I realised that my wife was looking out at us from Michael's bedroom window.

I had quickly wished Petra a good evening and headed for the house, waving her away casually and doing my best to make it look like we were just two people who had finished a banal chat, which we were really. Okay, maybe there was a little flirting in there, but it was harmless. And it was all from Petra, not me. I was just being nice and making conversation. All I had come outside for was the car manual. It wasn't my fault that I had bumped into her on the driveway before I could make it back in the house.

So why do I feel so sheepish now? I've returned to my study, and I want to close the door, but I feel as though I need to go upstairs and see Amy. She is probably wondering what we were talking about out there so I should probably tell her. Of course, I won't mention the fact that Petra complimented me on my aftershave or that she told me I looked good. I think I'll leave those bits out. But I will tell her that we briefly chatted about how Michael's lessons were going and that things sounded a little more promising regarding his end of year exams.

I should go up and say that. I should leave this study. I should talk to my wife. So why am I not doing that? For some reason, I feel nervous about having to go and explain myself. It was an innocent conversation. There's no need for me to tell Amy what we were discussing. Of course, I will do if she asks but if not then what is the point? It might look more suspicious if I do feel like I have to explain it. Then Amy might suspect that I find Michael's tutor attractive. I do, but that's not the point. I find several celebrities attractive too. It doesn't mean I have to feel bad about that and it doesn't mean that anything is going to happen there either.

In the end, I close my study door and re-take my seat at the desk. It was just a little chat between a parent and a tutor. There's no need to read anything into it and certainly no need to go and re-hash it all with my wife.

It was nothing. I should just forget about it.

So why can't I?

THE FIFTH LESSON

The police officers wore stern expressions when they visited the house. They had every right to do so because they were there on serious business. There is a time and place for smiling, but this was not it.

When the door opened, the homeowner looked surprised. She was a middle-aged woman, and she clearly hadn't been expecting to see the uniforms on her doorstep. Why would she? She was just a plain woman in a plain town with a plain family. She had a husband, she had two teenage girls, and she had a dog. There was nothing remarkable about her.

But the police weren't there for her. Nor were they there for her husband and they certainly weren't there for her dog. They were there to speak to one of her daughters.

They asked the mother if her eldest daughter was home and she nodded to confirm that she was. Then she stepped aside and allowed the officers in.

The front door closed, and it would be ten minutes before it opened again. When it did, the police officers stepped back outside but they were taking someone with them this time.

The sixteen-year-old girl had tears in her eyes as she was led towards the car in handcuffs. Her fourteen-year-old sister shouted at the officers and said words that a girl of her age should not be saying to anybody, let alone those responsible for upholding the law. The father made an appearance too, and he seemed only slightly more restrained than his youngest daughter was being.

But the mother was quiet. She wasn't arguing like the others on her doorstep were, nor was she crying like her child who was now being put onto the backseat of the police car. She was doing nothing but watching. That was because she was in shock.

She was in shock after finding out what her daughter had just been charged with.

The fifth lesson is that anybody could be guilty, even your own flesh and blood.

21

AMY

I asked Nick what he was talking about with Petra, but I didn't make a big deal of it. I had waited for him to come up to bed before broaching the subject, doing my best to make the question sound as carefree and casual as possible. It didn't work though. No sooner had he answered me then he had started to tease me about being jealous of the new woman around the house.

They had just spoken about Michael's progress, Nick said, and I believe him. What else would they have talked about? Maybe there was a little bit of emotion stirred up inside me from seeing my husband chatting alone with a pretty woman. But that's just silly. I'm forty for heaven's sake.

So why do I feel a little envious of Petra now?

It can't just be her looks. It's the way she made Nick smile on the driveway. I haven't seen him smile like that at me for a long time. We're a great couple and hardly ever argue, and I used to think that was a good thing. But maybe it means we have lost our spark. Maybe that's why his eyes don't light up around me as much as they do around her.

It's Michael too. He seems genuinely motivated and interested when she is around yet I have to work so hard to get anything out of him when it's just us two. I used to think that all mums had to put up with that from their teenage sons, but what if I'm wrong? Maybe Michael just doesn't say much to me because he finds me boring. Maybe he thinks we have nothing in common and can't see how engaging with me for more than two minutes at a time would be of any benefit to him.

Or maybe I'm just reading far too much into things like I always do.

Speaking of reading, I'm supposed to be doing that now. I have a paperback in my hand, and I'm trying to finish this chapter, but I can't quite manage it. I'm struggling to concentrate. Nick seems happy enough beside me, thumbing his way through his book. But my mind is far from the pages of this book and instead keeps drifting back to the Swedish woman who left this house a couple of hours ago. I can't quite put my finger on the cause of it, but I have an unsettled feeling in my stomach. Yet I have no reason to. Everything seems to be fine. Michael is finally revising. Bella seems happy. And Nick is still being Nick.

So what is making me feel so uneasy?

I let out a deep sigh and tell myself to concentrate on the words on the page. I just need to lose myself in the story. I just need to quieten my mind down a little.

I just need to stop thinking so damn much.

I'm barely two sentences further on in the book before my mind goes back to that sight of Nick and Petra on the driveway. The way she laughed. The way he smiled. The way they stood so close together.

I can't bring it up again with Nick because then he really will think that I'm jealous, which I am, even though there is nothing to be jealous about. But I can't help myself.

'Do you think Petra seems a little too good to be true?' I ask, closing my book and turning to look at my husband.

He frowns and stops reading and I wonder if I have just asked a ridiculous question.

'What are you talking about?' he replies in a tone that does suggest that it was a bad question.

'I just mean she's nice, she's a good teacher, she doesn't cost a fortune, and she is willing to come to us rather than making us take Michael to her. It all seems perfect, doesn't it?'

'And that's a problem because...?'

'It's not a problem. I'm just saying. It's all very convenient, isn't it?'

'Amy, I have no idea what you are getting at,' Nick says, closing his book and begrudgingly returning it to his bedside table.

'I'm just wondering why someone like her is doing this. She could be anything she wants to be. Why is she spending her time teaching secondary school kids GCSE

Maths in Nuneaton? Why did she leave Sweden to come here of all places? Why isn't she doing something more with her life?'

'Why don't you ask her?' Nick replies, returning my assault of questions with one of his own. And it is the obvious one. Why don't I just ask her? I could offer her a cup of tea after the next lesson and attempt to get to know her a little more then. But she might think that I'm strange for caring so much.

'It doesn't matter,' I say, and I pretend to go back to reading my book.

But Nick isn't buying it. He knows when I have a bee in my bonnet about something, and he knows I am not going to be able to concentrate on the story after I have just displayed such an interest in someone else's.

'Maybe she just really enjoys teaching. And maybe she likes the English way of life. Maybe she wanted something more than just being another blonde Swedish girl in Stockholm. Helping youngsters with their education is probably a little more fulfilling than being a model.'

'You think she could be a model?' I ask, closing my book quickly and looking at Nick.

'No, I just assumed that was what you were getting at,' he replies. 'You obviously think she could have been more than just a tutor.'

'I'm just curious about her, that's all,' I say, putting my book down too because there is nothing in there that is interesting to me as much as finding out more about this woman that I have invited into my home on a semi-regular basis.

'Are you sure you aren't a little jealous?' Nick asks, snuggling in closer to me and attempting to tickle me under my arm.

'No I'm not!' I reply, wriggling out of the way before he can get his hand in there and make me scream.

'You know I prefer brunettes,' Nick says before kissing me softly on the neck. 'Forty-year-old brunettes.'

I know what he is trying to do. He is just trying to make out that he finds me more attractive than Petra, which is frankly ridiculous. But I appreciate the attempt, and

I certainly appreciate the attention that I'm getting now. It has been a while since we were intimate. I haven't exactly made any attempts to break that dry spell myself, but it seems like it is about to end right now.

I reach for the lamp on the bedside table as Nick continues to kiss my neck. By the time the room is dark, he is already on top of me.

22

PETRA

I wish Nick was on top of me. I wish I could feel his strong arms holding me down, and I wish I could see those eyes of his looking down at me from above. I wish he was here right now.

I wish I was in that bed at his house instead of Amy.

But I'm not. I'm alone in my one-bedroom flat, and I only have my imagination to keep me company. My brain is the most important tool in my professional life, and it seems it is the most important one in my personal life too. But I've spent enough time living in my head. I just want to break out of it and really experience life.

No questions. No revision. No fantasies.

Just fun.

I wonder what Nick is doing right now. He might still be hard at work in his study. Maybe he is sitting on the sofa watching a movie. Or perhaps he is lying in bed with a good book.

He could be asleep. He might be talking to Amy.

Or maybe he is thinking about me.

The thought of it is thrilling, and I imagine that I might be right. I spent a few minutes talking to him before I left his house this evening and I wonder how many times he has replayed that conversation over in his head since then. I bet he is wondering if I like him. I bet he wants to know if I find him attractive for his age.

And I bet he wants me to touch him again.

A smile curls at the edges of my lips as I think about him lying in bed with his wife while thinking about me instead. It's amusing, and it's also exciting. I've had so much practise at living inside my own head all day, but I do find it fascinating to think about all the things that could be going on in other peoples. I'm already counting down until my next lesson with Michael. But it's not him that I want to see. It's his father.

But our next session isn't until Tuesday. That's four long days to get through before then. As far as Amy knows, I have other students and lessons to occupy my time before then. But I don't. I just told her that I did. That's what I told her so she would think that I'm just a polite, friendly and hardworking tutor who has many students and who is willing to travel to wherever the work is. She'll eventually find out the truth.

But by then, it will be too late.

23

AMY

It's Friday. The last day of the working week. The last day of school runs. The last day of rush hours. The last day of having to get out of bed early and stir my family into action. Two days of bliss before it all starts again. I'm ready for this weekend. But first I need to get through this final day.

I'm back at the school again, but I can't just drop the kids and leave like I usually do. I have to go inside today. I have to speak to one of the teachers.

Michael has already gone inside, but Bella is walking with me. I know that she would prefer to be alone, but I need her to show me where to go so that I can find my way to the staff room. That should be where I find her form tutor, Mrs Samson. Then all that will be left to do will be to have an awkward conversation and leave.

God, I wish it was the weekend already.

So much for my belief that Bella was a happy little soul. That belief had been shattered when she had walked into our bedroom last night after lights out. Fortunately, Nick and I had finished making love well before then otherwise it would have been very embarrassing for all parties. As it was, we had just been drifting off to sleep before Bella appeared in the doorway.

She had told the two of us that there was a girl in her class who had been teasing her recently. I asked her why she hadn't mentioned this before, and she had said that she thought it would have stopped by now. But it hadn't. Apparently, it had been going on for a while. And there was me thinking that Michael was the only one I had to worry about at school.

I had felt awful to hear that my daughter was being made to feel unhappy, and even worse for not picking up on that fact. But Bella had done a very good job of covering it up. She had always acted as if there was nothing wrong when I had picked her up and dropped her off, and she had still been dancing away to the pop videos in her bedroom every night, so I'd had no idea. But her veneer had finally cracked last night, and she had told us everything.

The girl is called Rebecca, and she is in Bella's form. Apparently, the teasing started after Bella had asked to go to the toilet one morning at registration. Rebecca had decided then that Bella had a problem and had started to tease her about it. She would say that Bella was going to wet herself when they were in class or on the playground, even though it wasn't true. Bella had ignored it initially, but gradually it had worn her down, and she was worried that everybody was going to believe it.

Nick told her to just ignore it because it is silly teasing, which of course it is, but I know it isn't as easy as that. Adults have no problem dealing with annoying peers, but children are different. They can be made to feel very bad about things, and it needs to be nipped in the bud before it can get any worse. I'm not sure I would go as far as to call it bullying yet, but it needs to stop, whatever it is. That's why I am going to speak to Mrs Samson today. It's time to put a stop to this before it gets any worse.

I look down at my daughter as we cross the playground, but she is happy to keep her own eyes on the concrete. I know that she will be feeling uncomfortable about having her mum walking with her into school, but I need her to show me where to go. I used to know this place like the back of my hand, but that was before it burnt down. Now I have no idea how to navigate my way around this school.

I've been inside a couple of times for parents' evenings, and that showed me how much has changed since I was a pupil here. Gone are the drab narrow corridors and claustrophobic classrooms and in their place are spacious and colourful rooms, all of which are now unfamiliar to me and anybody my age who once attended this very place themselves. I used to know all the shortcuts to get to where I needed to be, but now I'm as lost as any student starting on their first day here. All the rooms that used to hold so many memories for me have gone; replaced by rooms that look nicer but blank me with their unfamiliarity. There's no doubt that things have improved around here since I was in attendance and I'm glad that Michael and Bella don't have to freeze like I did through another long winter in a place that had a broken heating system. But it does feel strange to be treading on land that I walked over so many times before yet have absolutely no idea where I'm going.

'The staff room is just down there,' Bella says to me after we have gone through one of the entrance doors and found ourselves standing in a busy corridor.

I look down at the blue door at the end of the corridor and see a middle-aged man going through it behind a sea of uniforms who rush around with much more vigour and youth than that older figure possesses.

'Mrs Samson will be in there?' I ask my daughter, taking her word for it because I don't have much choice.

'I guess. Where else would she be?' Bella replies, and I take that as my cue to let her go before she feels too embarrassed to be standing beside me anymore.

'Okay, have a good day and we'll chat tonight,' I say to my daughter but she is already walking away and is quickly swallowed up by the bustling crowd of students within seconds.

Heading for the staff room at the end of the corridor, I can't help but notice all the strange looks I am getting from some of the kids that I am passing. None of them recognise me, and they are probably wondering if I'm going to be the next teacher to try and control them. Thank God I'm not. Judging by the behaviour of some of these kids, they require some serious taming. But that is a job for somebody far more patient than me.

I reach the door and hesitate for a moment before knocking on it. That delay gives the person on the other side of it the chance to open it themselves, and I am now face to face with a handsome but harassed secondary school teacher.

'Oh, hello,' he says when he notices me loitering outside the room that I shouldn't be anywhere near.

'Hi, erm, is Mrs Samson in there?' I ask, feeling like a nervous schoolgirl now that I am back in the presence of teachers and classrooms.

'Yeah. Sorry, you are?'

'I'm Amy. Bella Lever's mum. Mrs Samson is her form tutor.'

'Oh, right. Okay. One second.'

He pokes his head back in the door, and I hear him call out the name Sheila before he turns back to me with a smile.

'She'll be right out.'

'Thank you,' I say as I watch him rush away into the crowded corridor and off to start what will presumably be another long and tortuous day teaching the local youth.

As I wait for Mrs Samson to come out, or Sheila Samson as I have now learnt her full name to be, I think about how I can't wait to get back home this morning. Aside from this unexpected situation with Bella, last night ended up being pretty good. Nick and I were intimate for the first time in forever, and it was great. Even better than great, actually. It was fantastic. I'm not sure what had gotten into him, but all I know is that he certainly took my mind off my silly thoughts about Petra. Of course, with my brain being the way that it is, I did have one moment of paranoia in thinking that Nick might have been imagining her when he was on top of me, but I dismissed that for the nonsense that it is. My anxiety is always trying to find drama where there isn't any. Instead, it is time to focus on what is real. Bella needs my help now, and I am going to sort this out with her teacher. Then I am going to go home and get the house tidy. Then I'll be back here to pick the kids up at half three. And then finally it will be the weekend, and I'll spend most of my time cooking, cleaning and trying to find ways to entertain my family.

That's just what mums do. There's no need to complicate things with silly thoughts and worries.

No need at all.

24

NICK

I know I shouldn't feel bad. It's just what men do. I don't need to overcomplicate it.

So why do I keep thinking about it?

I recline in my chair, putting a little more distance between myself and the work that I haven't been able to concentrate on all morning. The reason for my lack of focus today is because of what happened last night. Amy and I were physical for the first time in a long time. But that's not the problem.

The problem is that I was thinking of Petra the whole time.

That in itself is probably no big deal. I'm sure Amy has imagined me as some hunky Hollywood actor over the years when we have been in bed, and that doesn't bother me one bit. I guess the difference is that the person I imagined myself being with is somebody who is actually a part of our lives. There's not much chance of Amy having a flirty chat with an A-list celebrity at our house, but how would I feel if she imagined herself with somebody who I know? I'm sure that I would feel pretty bad. That's how I know Amy would hate the fact that I was thinking of my son's tutor when I was in bed with her last night.

Fortunately, there is no way she is going to find out. My wife is capable of many things, but mind reading is not one of them. That's lucky or I'd probably be out on the street right now and begging to be let back inside. But the fact that Amy doesn't know that my mind wandered onto Petra doesn't mean I am absolved of all guilt. I feel troubled that I am thinking of Michael's tutor in this way. It's undoubtedly going to make me feel even more awkward when she comes for the next lesson, and I have to make small talk as if I didn't just imagine her like that.

The best way to avoid any more thoughts about her is for me to stay hidden away when she is here. I'll keep the study door closed and my mind on my work. Trying to decode a bug in a client's software is a sure-fire way to stop me thinking naughty thoughts.

But I don't want to hide away in here like some awkward teenager. This is my house; I should feel comfortable to be here no matter what. But that's not the real reason I would rather not lock myself away when Petra is around.

The real reason is that I know I will enjoy seeing her again.

Giving up on work for the moment, I leave my study and head for the fridge, deciding that food might offer a better distraction for me at this moment. I pull open the door and find the leftovers from last night's dinner. Lasagne. I don't bother reheating it.

As I tuck into the tasty dish, I decide that I will make sure that I am out of the house when Petra comes round to teach Michael. I'll go for a jog. It doesn't matter that I haven't been for a run in years. It's time to get back into the habit. I'll have to have a few practise runs first if I'm going to be able to last the time while Petra is around, but it will be worth it.

If I am out of the house, then I won't see her. If I don't see her, then I won't be attracted to her. And if I'm not attracted to her, then the image of her beauty will fade in my mind, and I won't find myself thinking about her when I am with Amy again.

See, I'm not such a bad husband after all. I am removing myself from a situation that could potentially be hazardous to my marriage. Not that anything would ever happen between the tutor and me. There's no chance of that.

No way.

But this will ensure it. Now we won't have any more little chats on the driveway. Now she won't smile at my jokes or touch my arm. And now I won't end up thinking about her instead of the woman that I am married to.

I've soon finished the lasagne, but I regret not heating it up. Maybe it would have been nicer that way. Oh well, it's no big deal. There are worse things to have regrets about.

Much worse.

25

AMY

I'm glad I was able to speak to Bella's form tutor. Mrs Samson is a pleasant woman, and she has assured me that she will have a word with the pupil in question and make sure that the teasing of my daughter stops before it gets any worse.

With my motherly duties taken care of for now at least, I am back home and having a little me time before they start all over again. I'm lying on the bed with a slice of cucumber over my eyes in an attempt to reduce the puffiness around them. This is something that I have unfortunately been forced to start doing now that I'm finding that my skin isn't as forgiving as it used to be. I used to laugh at the idea of women putting pieces of fruit on their face to make themselves look more youthful, but that was when I was young and enjoyed my skin's elasticity. Now I've hit forty, I'm falling into line like the rest of the middle-aged women out there.

I take a deep breath and tell myself that I will give it another five minutes before removing the green circles and rushing to the mirror to see if they have performed miracles on my tired face. But then I hear the sound of my husband in the downstairs hallway.

'I'm just going for a run!'

I remove one of the cucumbers and open a watery eye. Did I just hear him right? Did my husband say that he is going to go for a run? That would be the first time he's been for one all year. Maybe I'm not the only one grappling with my ageing body.

I remove the second cucumber and get up off the bed, calling it quits on my beauty regime to go and investigate my husband's attempts at his own. He doesn't miss a chance to tease me about my futile endeavours to stay young, so I'm not about to miss my chance to do the same to him.

'Did you say a run?' I ask as I look down the stairs and see my husband stretching by the front door. I recognise the clothes he is wearing from the last time he went for a jog, which was a long time ago because those same clothes have been lying at the bottom of the wardrobe in the spare bedroom for as long as I can remember. But he is wearing them now, and he has his trainers on too.

It really does look like he is going for a run.

'I just fancied it,' he says as he leans on the wall and lunges forward, activating muscles in his legs that have been dormant for as long as some volcanoes.

'I'm impressed,' I reply as I head down the stairs towards him. 'I thought your running days were over.'

'I figured I better get back into it,' Nick says as he switches legs and lunges again. 'If I spend any more time in that study, I think I'll morph into the desk.'

'How long are you going to be?' I ask, not because I need him back home anytime soon but rather because I'm worried about him overdoing it and being unable to walk for the upcoming weekend.

'Not long, just half an hour or so,' he replies, and he turns to the doorway, seemingly warmed up and ready to hit the tarmac.

'Okay, be careful,' I say as he opens the door. 'And don't pull anything.'

'I'll be fine,' he replies, flashing me a smile before stepping outside and closing the door behind him.

The silence in the house is welcome, and I have learnt to appreciate it when I get it. It will be over before I know it. Between Bella's music, Michael's video games and Nick's penchant for slamming doors, there aren't many times in my day when this house is quiet. But it is right now, and it is bliss.

I move through my peaceful home and reach the kitchen, where I head for the fridge with my heart set on having some of that leftover lasagne that I know is in there on the second shelf. But I'm disappointed when I see that there is no sign of it inside. Nick must have had it. Maybe that's why he's gone for a run.

The little pig scoffed the whole thing.

I close the fridge door, smirking at my husband's appetite. I don't mind really. It's probably for the best. I'd only have ended up eating most of it myself, and then I would have felt guilty all day. There isn't much point putting fruit on my eyes if I'm putting everything else in my belly.

I'm just about to start unloading the dishwasher when I remember that I wanted to look at something that one of my friends had been talking about in our WhatsApp group the other day. She had told me about this new holiday website that has some fantastic offers on, and she and her husband had just booked a twelve-night stay in Tenerife for a crazily low price. I'd been meaning to go online and have a look but haven't got around to it yet. Maybe now is my chance.

My own laptop is upstairs by my bed, but I decide that I can't be bothered to walk that far, so I go into Nick's study instead. I don't use his laptop much, but I know that it is a lot quicker than the ancient relic that I have as a personal device and I can't be bothered to sit and wait for ten minutes while it loads up. I'll just pop online on his while he is out running and see if I can spot any bargains for our summer holiday this year. He won't mind me using it, and he certainly won't mind if I tell him that I have found us a cheap deal to get some much-needed sun.

I sit down in his comfy office chair and enter the password on his laptop. It's the same one he uses for everything else. AMB1996. The first letter of my name, his two children's names and the year that we got together. He's such a sweetheart.

Or at least I thought he was.

I've just clicked on the tab to open up Google and start hunting for holidays, but it has brought up a page that he must have already had open instead. I recognise it instantly because I was on the same page myself not so long ago.

I see the blonde hair. I see the blue eyes. And I see that annoyingly perfect smile.

This is Petra's Facebook page.

Why is my husband looking at this?

THE SIXTH LESSON

Nobody believed her when she said she didn't do it. And why would they? The evidence was damning. She had been seen at the school that night. An empty jerry can had been found near the burnt school with her parent's address on. And her parents admitted their daughter was out that night, which meant she had no alibi.

She had to have done it.

Who else could it have been?

The police were convinced, which is why they refused to let her go until they got a confession. She never offered one of course, but under pressure to solve the serious crime, the evidence they did have was used against her.

It wasn't just the police who were confident that they had the guilty person. The public were too. The local newspaper was assured enough about the future conviction to put the perpetrator's face all over its front pages. The fire was big news. It wasn't every day that a whole school got burnt to the ground and it wasn't every day that an upstanding member of society burned along with it.

The interview room at that police station was an uncomfortable and trying place, but it wasn't much better than what would have been waiting for that poor girl if she had been on the outside. She was already the most hated person in town, and the punishment from the police was the least of her worries. Death threats had been posted through the letterbox of her parents' house, the same house that had been bombarded with insults and accusations, not to mention eggs, waterbombs and even bricks. It was clear that the family would have to leave the area when all of this was over, whenever that might be. But there were those for whom it would never be over. They had lost so much in the fire that nothing could ever make things right again.

It really was a terrible time for everyone in the town. But it was worst for the teenage girl sitting opposite the police offers in that interview room. She was hated, she was vilified, and she was condemned.

She was also completely innocent.

The sixth lesson is don't believe everything you read in the papers.

26

MICHAEL

This lesson has been a little different from the first couple. That's because we're over half an hour in and Petra hasn't even asked me a question yet. The textbooks are still closed, and I haven't learnt a thing. Not that I'm complaining. How could I? I'm being quizzed about my personal life by a stunning Swede. This is much better than discussing probabilities.

So far, Petra has asked me about myself, which makes a change from how she had been during our first lesson when she had been all about studying. I guess she has relaxed a little now that she feels like she has impressed my parents enough to prove that she is the right person for the job. She probably thinks that I have been reporting back to them after our sessions together with feedback on how things are going and how much I'm learning. But I'm not. Not really. Mum and Dad ask me how it is going, and I say it's good, but I'm not talking about the work. I'm talking about the fact that I get to sit with a woman like this for two hours.

Petra could never ask me another Maths question again, and I would still tell my parents that she was the best teacher I have ever had. But today it is me that is doing the teaching and her doing the learning. Petra wants to know as much about me as possible, and I'm only too happy to tell her.

'So you play a lot of video games?' she asks me with one of her elbows leaning on the cover of the GCSE Maths textbook.

'Yeah, loads,' I reply, perhaps a little too quickly. 'I mean not loads, just now and again.'

I don't want to come off as some hermit who sits in his bedroom all day and only interacts with a games console. It's hardly going to be attractive to her, even if that is all I do.

'What do you play?' she asks me, and I wonder if she is genuinely interested or just being nice.

'Mainly FIFA. I love football.'

'Cool. We'll have to have a game sometime.'

'Yeah, that would be awesome!'

I say that a little too enthusiastically and quickly clear my throat. I pretend that the high pitch of my voice was caused by something stuck in there rather than my excitement at playing my favourite game with my crush. The guys at school would really be jealous if they found out Petra had been in my bedroom.

'Which football team do you support?' she asks me, and I still can't believe my luck that I'm spending my whole Maths lesson talking about things that I actually enjoy.

'Aston Villa,' I reply. 'I go to loads of matches.'

'With your dad?'

I'm caught off guard by the question and quickly try to figure out what the best answer would be. Yes, I do go to the games with my dad but admitting so might remind her of my age, and I'm trying my best to come across as an adult. I could just say that I go with my friends. That would make me seem more mature. But then what if she talks to Dad and finds out that he is the one who takes me to matches? Then she will know I have been lying to her. Then again, why would she be talking to Dad about football?

'Michael?'

I realise I haven't answered her.

'I go with my friends. We get the train together and usually go out afterwards.'

'Go out?' she repeats, eying me a little suspiciously. 'As in drinking?'

Of course we don't go out drinking. We're sixteen. We wouldn't get in anywhere. But I'm trying to seem older, so I have to keep it going.

'Yeah.'

'You can get into pubs?'

The questions keep coming so I have no choice but to keep answering them as best I can.

'Yeah. Some of them. I have a fake ID, but I never have to use it. I guess I look old enough without it.'

I'm lying about the fake ID, and I'm lying about looking old enough. I have never tried getting served in a pub with my mates, and that is for one simple reason. I don't want to be laughed at by the landlord. But Petra doesn't need to know that.

'Cool. So you like going out for a pint, do you?'

'Oh yeah, I love a pint,' I reply, nodding and trying to look like a sophisticated drinker, even if the only pints I drink consist of Coca Cola while playing video games at 2 am.

'I'm more of a wine drinker myself,' Petra tells me, and I decide I need to be too.

'Yeah, I don't mind a wine,' I say, but I worry I have pushed my luck a little when I get the next question.

'Really? What's your favourite wine?'

'Erm...,' I do my best to try and remember what wine I have heard my parents talking about over the years. But I can't quite recall it.

My eyes quickly scan the kitchen until they land on the wine rack in the corner. I can just about make out the label on the bottle on the top shelf.

'Sharaz?' I say, unsure if I have read the bottle right from this distance.

‘Shiraz?’ Petra asks, and I guess that must be what I mean.

‘Yeah,’ I reply, nodding confidently. ‘But me and my friends call it Sharaz. Long story.’

I bat the air dismissively as if there really is a long story about why I called it Sharaz. It’s better than admitting that I have absolutely no bloody clue what I am talking about right now.

‘Well, I am impressed. I didn’t start drinking until I was eighteen, but I can see that you are already way ahead of me there.’

I feel a warm glow inside and do my best to stop a massive smile breaking out across my face. Petra is impressed.

I have impressed her.

‘So how did your mum and dad meet?’ she asks me.

I’m surprised by the sudden change in the direction of the conversation. I thought we were talking about me, and I was rather hoping that I would have more opportunities to impress her. Never mind. This is still better than talking about Maths.

'They met at school,' I say. 'When they were my age.'

I cringe because I have just reminded Petra that I am sixteen and I have spent the last half an hour trying to make her forget about that. But it's too late now. I've done it. Fortunately, Petra doesn't seem to mind or even notice. Instead, she just keeps asking me about Mum and Dad.

27

PETRA

I've been feigning interest in Michael's life for the last half an hour, but now we are finally talking about what I really want to get into.

Amy and Nick's relationship.

Their son has already told me that they met in their last year of school. That means they have been together for their whole adult life. I thought that was just something that couples did in movies.

'Wow, so they have been together since they were sixteen?' I ask, raising my eyebrows to telegraph to Michael that I find that surprising.

'Yeah, pretty much,' he replies. 'They got married at twenty-two, had me at twenty-four. Pretty young, huh?'

'Very young,' I reply, and Michael seems impressed that we agree on something else. Of course, those ages aren't young to get married and have children. Not if the people involved are in love. But I pretend they are to my student because I want him to think that we are both on the same page. That will be the best way for me to keep extracting information from him.

'Do you have a boyfriend?' Michael suddenly asks me, and I can tell by his facial expression that he probably meant to think it rather than actually blurt it out.

I hold off on giving him an answer for a moment, more to tease him than anything else, before I finally put him out of his misery.

'Nope, I'm single,' I say breezily, letting him know that my freedom is something that I enjoy.

'The best way to be,' Michael advises, nodding his head as if he is some sage of the dating game. 'You have to enjoy life before you settle down.'

I manage to hold in the laugh that is threatening to leave me and nod my head too. This kid is sixteen, yet he's trying to make out like he has loved and lost. The only thing he loves is his video games, and the only thing he has lost is his homework.

But I appreciate his effort to impart some wisdom onto me.

Of course, it should be me who is imparting the wisdom on him, yet thirty minutes into the lesson and I haven't even begun to teach him any of the things that his parents are paying me to do. Not that it's a problem. I hardly expect him to go and complain to his mum and dad about his lack of learning here today. I'm sure he is enjoying our conversation a lot more than he would be if we were back on probabilities again.

'So what are your parents' hobbies?' I ask, making sure the flow of information is still going to keep coming from across the table.

'Drinking wine,' Michael suggests lazily, and I laugh. I'm sure he meant it as a joke, but he seems a little surprised by my reaction, so maybe he was being serious. 'Dad likes football like I said. And mum watches TV.'

I smile because he has answered the questions with about as much enthusiasm as I would have expected a teenage son to speak about their parents with. But I just know that he is dying to get the conversation back onto himself again. He'll be thinking of all the different ways he can try and impress me with his maturity some more. I will go back to asking him about himself shortly. But I just have a couple more things I want to know first.

'Do you think your parents are happy?' I ask, keeping the tone of my voice light to deflect away from the weight of the question I have just asked.

Michael looks a little uncomfortable and shifts in his seat so I allow my gaze to lower to the Maths book in front of me as a way to remind him that there is something else we could be talking about instead.

'I guess so,' he replies, making sure my gaze is returned to him and not the multitude of GCSE questions in that book. 'I never hear them arguing.'

'That's good. Although some would say...' I allow my sentence to drift off. 'Never mind.'

'What?' Michael asks, intrigued by what I might be thinking.

'Well, it's just that some people might say that if couples don't argue, then it shows a lack of passion in the relationship. But I think that's a load of rubbish.'

Michael doesn't seem so sure, so I press on.

'Would you say that they have passion?'

'What do you mean?' he asks me, and he looks every bit of his age right now. I make sure that I remind him of it too.

'Sorry, forget about it. You're sixteen. You don't know about all of that stuff yet.'

I say it in a tone that lets him know that I don't mean it in a disparaging way. But I want him to feel bad, at least just a little. As I let my words sink in, I flip open the textbook in front of me and pretend to be getting ready to finally start the lesson.

'You mean sex?' he asks me, and the word is enough to get me to look up from the book.

I allow my silence to give him his answer.

'They have sex,' he continues. 'I heard them the other night actually. At least I heard the start of it. I put my headphones in quickly before they could really get going.'

I smile at how much Michael is blushing as he says all of this. No teenager wants to talk about their parents in this way, but he is obviously trying to make sure that I know he is aware of those kinds of things, and I appreciate his effort.

'Wow, lucky them,' I say. 'I guess being married isn't so bad.'

Michael laughs, and I bet he is thinking about how he can tell all his friends at school about how he got to talk about sex with his tutor. I'm sure he has already shown them a picture of me. I bet he has been on my Facebook page. Why else would he have asked me for my surname last week?

'Right, we better get some work done,' I say, finding the page that I want in the book.

'Is there anything else you want to know?' Michael asks hopefully, trying to put off revising for one more minute if he can. But I was expecting this.

I pretend to think about it for a moment before I ask him the question that I had already had in mind before he sought it.

'Which night was it when you heard your mum and dad?'

Michael thinks about it for a second, probably wondering why it matters. But it does matter. It matters to me.

'Thursday,' he replies. 'Yeah, I'm pretty sure it was Thursday.'

'Cool,' I say, doing my best to suppress the grin that is trying to break out on my face.

That was the answer that I was hoping to hear. That's because Thursday was the last time I was here. It was the night I spoke with Nick on the driveway.

I imagine it was the reason why he was feeling so frisky that evening.

28

AMY

I'm sitting on Bella's bed watching my daughter run through some dance routine that she has just learnt on YouTube, but my mind is elsewhere. It's downstairs on the woman sitting at my kitchen table, as well as out on the streets where my husband is running. I might be being silly, but I can't help it.

I'm worried that something is going to happen between my husband and the tutor.

Bella's attempts at breakdancing are not enough to distract my wandering thoughts. Nick was looking at Petra's Facebook page in his study. Why else would he be doing that unless he was interested in her? I know I looked at her page too, but that is different. I was looking because I was a curious parent wanting to find out a little more about the person teaching my child. I very much doubt that was the reason why he found himself on that same page.

Now he is out running, which is something that he has only started to do since she started coming around. Is that what's motivating him? Is he trying to get in shape to look better in front of her? Is he using exercise as a way to try and impress her?

The fact that he is out of the house while she is here should be a good thing, but even that is making me a little paranoid. He could have gone for a run at any point today. Why has he gone now? Does he not want to be here when she is? If so, why not?

Is it because he is worried about what he might do if he sees her again?

'Mum, watch!' Bella cries, and I return my focus to my child. I've seen a million of these dances over the years, and I should enjoy them while they last because it's only a matter of time until she doesn't want me anywhere near her bedroom anymore. I should also be glad that she is in better spirits than she was last week when she came into my bedroom in the middle of the night and told me about the girl who had been teasing her. That seems to have been resolved since I spoke to Mrs Samson. Bella has said there had been no teasing since.

'Very good darling,' I say as I watch my daughter do some weird thing with her arms. God knows which celebrity has come up with this routine, but I imagine that I'm not the only parent in the world to be subjected to watching their child performing it tonight.

As Bella keeps dancing, my mind returns to the people outside of this room. I just can't help worrying about the fact that something might happen between Nick and Petra. But he wouldn't do that, would he?

Could he hurt me again?

I know that all my jealousy and anxiety stems from the fact that Nick has strayed before. It was ten years ago, but that doesn't mean I have ever fully recovered from it. It happened with a woman he used to work with back when he was still office-based. I saw a message flash up on his phone when he was in the shower one night. He must have forgotten to take his mobile in the bathroom with him like he usually did so I had been able to see what had just arrived on his device.

It was from a woman called Tina. It was a photo. And it had two kisses beneath it.

Using the code that he had told me about before, I unlocked the message and kept hold of the device until my husband had emerged from the bathroom. Then I had told him Tina had been in touch.

I had seen his face drop when I handed the phone to him. But that had been nothing compared to how he had reacted when I had demanded to know who she was.

He had got defensive. He had got angry. And he had got rude. But I had refused to drop it until he told me. In the end, he confessed to everything.

How he had been stupid. How he had been drunk. How he had been meaning to put a stop to it. How it had only happened because he spent all day with her at work. How the arrival of Bella had meant that there hadn't been much time for us. Most of all, he had told me how he was sorry, and he was never going to do anything like this again.

It had taken me a long time, but I had eventually forgiven him. I had told him that he had to leave his job and that woman and he did, and that is how he had ended up working from home. His new company told him about how he could work remotely, and he said it sounded perfect, which I had to agree with. Having him at home all day was one way of making sure nothing like that ever happened again. A decade on and those wounds are still there but buried deep.

But seeing that profile page open on his laptop the other day has sent me into a tailspin.

I haven't spoken to him about it yet. How can I? It's not as if he has been receiving messages from Petra. He has just been checking out her photos on social media. I don't want him to think that I'm so crazy that I won't allow him to browse the internet anymore. But why did it have to be her page?

Why did it have to be the woman who is in our house right now?

I regret not hiring Sue to be Michael's tutor. Then I wouldn't have had all these worries. There would have been zero chance of Nick being tempted if we had hired her, but there would have been zero chance of getting Michael to sit down and study with her too. I try to keep my anxiety at bay by telling myself that I am doing the best thing for my son, and it is only for a few more weeks until his exams come around. Besides, just because Nick might fancy Petra, it doesn't mean that she fancies him. He is twelve years older than her. I doubt she would be interested even if he was.

So why don't I feel better about things?

Bella keeps dancing while my mind keeps running.

Somewhere on those streets, Nick is doing his own kind of running.

29

NICK

You can't beat the endorphins that you get from a good run. I've been out here pounding the tarmac for forty minutes, and I feel great. My heart rate is up, my adrenaline is spiking, and the dopamine hit is making me feel better than I have felt in months. I can't believe I stopped doing this. I should never have quit running. At least I've got back into it again now. It's the best way of making yourself feel good naturally.

Okay, so maybe the second-best way.

I'm trying not to think about that other thing that people do to get a natural high. One, because I don't get to do that so much these days and two, I don't get to do it with the people that I want to.

Picking up the pace, I turn the corner at the top of the street and move onto flatter ground. I like going this way because of the hill that I am forced to climb, but I'm glad that I have reached the top now. I'm over halfway, and it won't be long until I'm back at home with my feet up. By that time Petra will have left, and I won't have to worry about bumping into her again.

I'm not the perfect husband, but I'm trying.

I haven't cheated on Amy since my mistake with Tina ten years ago. While I like to think that proves that I have learnt my lesson and have become a better husband, I am also aware that I haven't exactly been tested in all that time. I have worked from home ever since I left that office where the fling with Tina had begun, which means I have hardly been around another woman besides Amy since then. We have a few friends that we meet up with on occasion, but I have never looked at them in the same way that I looked at my former colleague, so I have never been tempted at all.

Not once.

Until now.

Petra is the first woman that I have been around since Tina who has made me feel like I did back then.

Alive.

That is why I am out of the house now. I need to avoid her while she is around so that I stop having those thoughts and feelings. Give it a few weeks and she will be gone, and then I can go back to normal because normal for me does not involve running up a damn hill on a cold Tuesday night.

The only problem is that her lessons with Michael last for two hours and I can't realistically keep running for that amount of time. Even in my fittest days, which were a long time ago, I could never have hoped to keep jogging for that long. That means I am going to have to go home while she is still there. It shouldn't be a problem if she is in the kitchen. I can just go through the front door and straight upstairs. I missed her arriving at the house, and I will stay up there so that I miss her leaving.

Easy.

I feel a slight pang of regret that I won't get to see her today, but it's that feeling which tells me how important it is that I stick to my plan. I used to have those feelings when I would drive into the office and see Tina and look where that got me. That's why I need to nip it in the bud now before it gets out of hand again.

I keep running but suddenly burst out laughing as I go. That's because it has just occurred to me that all of this is completely ridiculous. Just because I find Petra attractive it doesn't mean that she thinks the same way about me. So what if I see her? So what if we talk again? How could it lead anywhere if she has no interest in me?

But thinking like that makes me feel a little deflated. It's like a reminder of the fact that I am middle-aged now and not as handsome as I once was. I'm no gargoyle by any means, but my hair is thinner, and the weight has accumulated around my waist much more than it used to. I'm sure Petra would have fancied me when I was her age but now? Probably not.

But then I think about how she complimented me on the driveway. How she flicked her hair and smiled at me. How she touched my arm. I might be getting older, but I still know what body language to look out for. She wouldn't have touched me if she didn't like me.

She reduced the distance between us because she wanted to.

I suddenly find that I am running faster now, and I know exactly why that is. It's because of the energy that comes with the thought of thinking that a woman like Petra might actually be interested in a guy like me. Considering I spend all day stuck on my own in a study in a plain house in the suburbs of a small town, such a thing as that is extremely exciting.

Would I be this thrilled if I got out more? Probably not.

Forcing myself to slow down a little, I make myself remember why it is that I now spend so much time at home. I don't work in an office anymore because I made a mistake. This is the best way to ensure that that mistake never happens again. And there was no chance of it ever happening again.

Not until we invited her into our home.

This is my fault. I suggested Petra to Amy. I was the one who printed her profile off the internet. I was shocked when my wife agreed to try her but pleased at the same time. But I was naïve. I honestly thought that we could have a beautiful woman come into our home and it wouldn't make things difficult. But I was wrong. If I'm feeling like this, then I wonder if Amy is feeling like it too. I saw her looking out of the window at the two of us the other night. And she has been asking questions about Petra when we are together in bed. I guess she is aware that there is a risk to our happy marriage again.

I feel bad for Michael and his studies, but I know what I have to do. I'm going to tell Amy to let her go. If she asks why, then I will have to tell her the truth and say that I am attracted to her. I expect she would appreciate my honesty. I can't keep up with these stupid runs every time she comes around. I'll end up giving myself a hernia at best or a heart attack at worst. We can find Michael another tutor. Sue can do the job. I know my son won't like it, but he'll understand one day.

He'll understand when he is married.

He'll understand that people make mistakes and they have to do everything they can to avoid making them again.

30

MICHAEL

This is bullshit. As if having to get up early and go to school all day wasn't bad enough, my parents have just told me that tonight's lesson with Petra is going to be my last. They want to change my tutor.

They want Sue to teach me instead.

I asked them why but they didn't give me an answer that made any sense, just some rubbish about how they didn't think she was the right person for the job after all and they wanted somebody with more experience. But that explanation is crazy. I get on well with Petra, and she has taught me things since I have been working with her. Okay, so maybe she could have taught me a lot more, but I like the fact that she likes to ask personal questions before we start with the work. I bet Sue wouldn't do that. I bet it would be straight down to studying with her, which is why I would be bored and end up taking none of it in.

Mum and Dad just don't get it. I don't just struggle to learn things because I'm slow. I struggle because I have no connection with the person teaching me them. But I have that connection with Petra. I like her. She's funny, she's polite, and she's the first teacher I've had that I feel I can relate to in some way. I'm sick of crusty old lecturers barking orders at me and expecting me to engage with them. I need somebody younger and cooler, and I had that.

But now it is over.

Mum and Dad have said they want tonight's session to go ahead as normal, but then they will let Petra know that her services are no longer required when it is over. They have told me not to say anything to her so that her performance isn't affected, but I bet it's just because they don't want things to be awkward. I'm wondering why they haven't just let her go already, but I'm guessing it is because Sue isn't available to start until next week and they don't want to waste a session when my exams are looming on the horizon. But how do they expect me to concentrate now? I feel like telling Petra myself when we are alone, and then they will be sorry. It will be embarrassing for them to have to explain that they were using her for one more lesson while they are waiting for the next tutor to become free.

I'm sitting in my bedroom, but I'm so mad that I can't even be bothered to turn on the PlayStation. I'm not going to see Petra again after tonight.

Ever.

I feel like I've been punched in the stomach. So what if it's just a stupid crush? I can't help it. I like her. And so what if Mum and Dad know about it. I'm pretty sure they do know based on how I reacted when they gave me the news half an hour ago. I tried to pretend that I was angry because I enjoy the sessions, but they surely saw through it. They know that I'm mad because I like Petra and don't want to stop seeing her. But I'm not embarrassed. Why should I be? And does it really matter if I fancy my tutor? Why should my parents care as long as I am studying?

As if this wasn't bad enough, I'm going to have to tell my friends that Petra has been replaced by Sue. They are going to find that absolutely hilarious. They won't be jealous of me anymore then. They'll make fun of me and why wouldn't they? I would do it if it happened to one of them.

There has to be more to this. I can't believe that they would decide to change my tutor for no good reason. I don't believe all that nonsense about her not being experienced enough. She reads me questions out of a textbook, and I try and answer them. How experienced does she need to be? I rack my brains for another explanation as to why they seem so keen to get her out, but I can't come up with anything. But I do know one thing.

This was Mum's idea.

She did most of the talking when they told me downstairs, which means that she must be the one pushing for this. Dad didn't say much, not that he ever does when it comes to talking about something other than I.T. or football, but he seemed in agreement. Petra has to go.

Maybe something has happened? Maybe Petra said or did something to upset them? But I don't see how that is possible.

She literally walks through the front door, sits with me for two hours and then leaves. There's no way she could have offended them or upset them in any way.

What if Mum and Dad were listening in on our lessons? I try to figure out if that was possible. Maybe that would explain it. Perhaps they heard Petra asking questions about them.

Oh god, is that it? I told Petra that Mum and Dad had sex last week.

That must be it!

This is my fault!

I shake my head and blame myself for talking my way out of a good situation. I could have spent four hours a week with Petra for the next several weeks until my exams. Who knows what could have happened between us during that time? We would have got to know each other better. I might have been able to make her like me.

I might have even got her to kiss me.

But now those dreams are gone.

As if Mum and Dad were eavesdropping on our private conversations. That is so unfair. I hate living here. I shouldn't have to put up with this.

Then again, maybe I don't have to. I'm not a child anymore. I'm sixteen, which means that I'm an adult. I should be able to see who I want when I want. If it can't be under this roof then so be it. It will have to be under someone else's. What if I continue my lessons with Petra elsewhere? Mum and Dad won't be able to say no to that. They won't even have to know about it. I guess the only obstacle is payment. I need to find out how much Petra charges and see if I can get the money myself. It will be worth it to spend more time with her. It will be worth it to keep making my friends jealous.

And it will be worth it if I eventually get that kiss.

THE SEVENTH LESSON

The exams took place in an unfamiliar hall, but that was all that was different about them. The questions on the pages were still the same, as was the amount of time given to answer them and the significance of the results when they were finally collected and marked. The burning down of the school had meant that pupils of Sharpbell High had been forced to take their exams later than the pupils in the rest of the country. Arrangements had needed to be made with the neighbouring school to accommodate them and give the displaced pupils the best chance at finishing their school careers without distraction. The sports hall at Maxwell High was the setting for the GCSE exams that summer, and while the surroundings had changed, everything else was the same.

The students sat in rows, their pens moving across the white papers that had been opened out on to wooden desks. Those desks were covered in the inky graffiti from all the students who had sat there before them.

Some of the messages on the desks offered hope and encouragement.

'Just one more exam and then I'll be free.'

'No more school. Yessss!

'Screw this place. I'm out of here!'

Other messages were more negative.

'I have no idea what I am doing.'

'Oh my god I'm going to fail.'

'HELLLPPPP MEEEEE!'

And some messages were just plain obscene.

The thing that bonded them all together was that they had been written by people going through a shared experience. It was the experience of taking an exam that could go on to have a big impact on the rest of their lives.

Everybody who should have been there that day was in their seats and answering the questions except for one. That missing student was sitting at home in her bedroom counting down the days until she was due to appear in court charged with crimes of manslaughter and arson.

The girl who had caused the fire was absent from the sports hall that day, which was unfair. It was unfair because she was innocent.

The people who had really caused that fire sat in that hall and answered the questions on the papers while looking forward to an exciting life beyond the confines of school.

The seventh lesson is that life isn't fair.

31

AMY

I feel better now that I have made the decision. Petra will finish her lesson with Michael tonight, and then I will pay her, thank her and tell her that we will, unfortunately, have to bring the lessons to an end. I'm going to try and keep my reasoning as vague as possible, but if she pushes me for answers, which she is entitled to do, then I will say that there has been a problem with my job and we need to save money. That means we are unable to keep paying her and she isn't going to work for free so she will accept it and be on her way. At least that is how I see it going in my mind. In reality, it will probably be much more awkward than that.

Michael wasn't happy about it although I didn't expect him to be. But it's not up to him. I am doing what is best for this family. The fact that Nick agreed with me tells me that this is the best thing for us all.

It would be nice to be able to trust my husband around a pretty woman, but I can't help the way that I feel. The scars from that betrayal a decade ago are still there, and they cut me deep. I should never have chosen a tutor like Petra because it has brought all those old feelings back to the surface.

The jealousy. The bitterness. The constant comparing myself to another female. I know nothing has happened between them but witnessing that brief conversation on the driveway was enough to tell me that I'm still feeling delicate about seeing Nick with a woman. With Petra out of the way then I can bury those feelings away again and hopefully they will stay there for at least another decade.

It's not unhealthy but screw it.

I know it is sad that I feel this way. I shouldn't go into a blind panic just from seeing another woman smile at my husband or because I have found a profile page open on his laptop. But I wasn't always this way. If that thing had never happened with Tina, then I would have just been a normal wife. As it is, I always feel like I have to be on my guard.

It's not that Nick is a bad husband. He isn't. Apart from that one brief and regrettable mistake, he has been nothing but kind, loving and compassionate. He is also a great father to Michael and Bella. I didn't want to throw away a lifetime of love and memories over one stupid mistake, and I'm glad that I didn't. But staying together has meant that things can never be as simple and innocent as they were back before he did what he did.

I feel bad that Michael has to suffer for this. If I genuinely believed that there was no other way of him getting the help he needs for his exams, then I would have had to put up with Petra being here for a little while longer. But I'm convinced that Sue can do just as good a job as the Swedish woman, if not better. The older woman certainly has more experience so that can't hurt. The difficulty now will be getting Michael to give her a chance, but I might have a way around that. I'm surprised I didn't think of it sooner. It was actually

Nick's idea, but I'm going to take some of the credit for it too. After tonight's lesson and after Petra has left, my husband and I will tell Michael that if he knuckles down and works hard with his new tutor, then we will pay for him and Nev to attend the big E-sports Festival in London at the end of the year. Apparently, it is the hottest ticket in town for fans of video games and all the new releases are expected to be unveiled as well as a whole host of other things that mean nothing to me but will presumably excite my son beyond belief. Tickets aren't cheap, but they will be his reward if he gives these next few weeks his all and does his best in his exams.

That is all we ask of him as parents.

I'm sure he will see it that way too.

The only thing left to do now is to break the news to Petra. I feel bad because she seems to be a genuinely nice woman and Michael tells me her lessons are great. But I have to put my mental health first. I will feel better when she is gone because I won't be that crazy woman again who has to check up on my husband to make sure that he isn't doing something that he shouldn't be. She would probably be mortified if she knew the truth that I am worried about something happening between her and Nick. I'm sure she thinks he is too old for her and probably doesn't look at him in that way at all. But it's not her that I'm worried about.

It's him.

I have to trust my gut on this one. I pride myself on always doing what I feel is best for my family, and this feels like this is the best thing to do.

Only time will tell if I am right.

32

PETRA

Something is troubling Michael. I can sense it. I haven't been teaching him for long, but I have spent enough time with him to notice when he is behaving a little differently with me, and he is definitely doing that now. He has been much quieter for a start. He also seems even more nervous than he usually is. I always put this down to him being uncomfortable because he was trying to impress me, but there is clearly something else going on now, and I'd like to get to the bottom of it before our lesson continues.

'Is everything alright?' I ask him, interrupting his train of thought as he sits in front of me and tries to work out the answer to the Maths question that I just asked him.

I expect him to lie and say yes, which will make me need to probe a little further. But I'm surprised when he answers me honestly.

'No, not really,' he replies, putting his pen down and looking up at me.

'What is it?' I ask, hoping that it's nothing to do with my teaching skills.

'Mum and Dad want me to have a different tutor.'

What? That was the last thing that I was expecting to hear.

'Really? Why?'

'I don't know. They said something about wanting somebody with more experience.'

'I have plenty of experience,' I say, slightly offended that I have to defend my credentials.

'I know you do. And I think you're great. But they said they have made up their mind.'

I bite my tongue as I think this through. There must be more to it than this. The experience thing is a ridiculous reason, and I'm sure Michael knows it as well as I do.

'Why haven't they said anything to me?' I ask him, thinking back to how welcoming Amy was when I arrived at the house this evening.

'They didn't want to spoil tonight's lesson. But they are going to tell you afterwards.'

I shake my head, annoyed at the deception from my customers. But they were right to leave it until after the lesson to tell me. I'd have left beforehand if they had given me the news then.

'I don't understand. I thought you were enjoying our lessons?' I say to Michael, playing the victim even though I know this has nothing to do with him.

'I do. I told them that, but they wouldn't listen. They just said it was for the best.'

I rack my brains for the real reason behind this. Of course I had been expecting to get the boot at some point but not this soon. I had so much to accomplish here before then, and I'm not talking about helping Michael with his revision.

'There must be something else,' I say, thinking out loud. 'Have you got any ideas?'

Michael suddenly looks sheepish, so I press him for answers.

'What?'

'I wonder if they overheard us talking the other day,' he says. 'About how I heard them in bed.'

I do recall Michael telling me about hearing his mum and dad being intimate the other night, as well as my comments on the matter. Perhaps he is right. Perhaps they did overhear us talking about them. I could see why Amy and Nick would get annoyed by that. Nobody would want their child's tutor hearing about what they got up to in their bedroom.

'You really think that's what it is?' I ask him.

Michael shrugs, and at that moment he looks every bit of his sixteen years of age. Just a confused, frustrated and helpless teenager being forced to deal with his parents' latest decision regarding his life. One day he will get to move out and be his own person, but for now, he is as trapped as every child living under their guardians' roof.

'Do you think I should go and have a word with your mum and dad?' I suggest, even though I have no intention of doing such a thing. I'm not going to go begging for my job. If anyone should be doing the begging, then it is them. And they will. All in good time.

'No,' Michael says quickly. 'Then they will know that I've told you.'

'Of course, I don't want to get you in any trouble,' I say, trying to sound nice but really saying it to make Michael feel his age.

'I won't get in trouble!' he replies in exactly the defensive manner that I expected.

'It's okay, I won't say anything,' I tell him, taking a moment to decide on my next move. I could do as I am supposed to and finish this lesson, then make my way to the front door where Amy will give me the news and send me on my way with my last payment. Or I could sabotage this last lesson and teach Michael some unnecessary things which will make his performance in the exam worse. But that would just be getting back at him rather than his parents, and they are the ones who want to get rid of me.

'I have an idea,' Michael says, surprising me with his input. 'I was thinking that I could come to your place and study instead of you coming here. My parents wouldn't have to know.'

I like the sound of that idea a lot, but I can't make it obvious right away. I have to pretend to Michael that I am thinking about it. But my delay only makes him try and convince me even more.

'I have some money. I could pay you myself,' he says, and it seems Michael isn't as far off being his own person as I had thought.

'I don't know if that's a good idea,' I reply. 'If your mum and dad think you will be better off with someone else, then I should respect that.'

'It's not up to them,' Michael says, with a fair amount of passion in his voice. 'It's my education. I should be the one who decides what is best. And I know that you are a much better tutor than anyone else they could get me.'

I'm flattered by my student's endorsement of me. What he means is that I'm better looking than anyone else that his parents could get for him. But I appreciate it nonetheless.

'I do need the money,' I lie, allowing my body language to depict me as the inferior one at this table for the first time since we sat down.

'Then it's decided,' Michael says with a big grin on his face. 'You'll still be my tutor. I'll come to you. My parents won't have to know a thing about it.'

I smile and say that sounds wonderful. I don't tell him that his parents are going to find out about it though. I don't want to ruin his happiness. They will find out. But it won't be because he lets slip about it. They will find out because I will tell them. But not yet. This will force me to change my plans slightly, but I can make this work in my favour. Just because I'm not in the house anymore, it doesn't mean that I can't learn more about this happy little family.

I'm so excited by what is to come that I can barely concentrate on the textbook for the rest of the lesson. But Michael doesn't seem to mind.

He really is a great student.

33

AMY

No one likes having an awkward conversation. We spend so much time trying to avoid them. It's the reason we don't walk past a particular person's desk in the office or make sure not to make eye contact with a stranger in a lift. Awkward conversations are something to be dodged at all costs. But there's no avoiding this one.

'Can I have a quick word?' I ask Petra before she can get her coat on and head for the door. Her lesson with Michael has just finished, and now I need to deliver the news to her that there will be no more. I feel bad for doing this and even worse because she will have no idea that it is coming, but my mind is made up. I just hope she takes it well.

'Yeah, sure,' Petra replies, displaying a dazzling smile that I'm sure has broken many hearts over the years.

I lead her into the living room but purposely don't take a seat on the sofa because I don't want the tutor to do the same and get comfortable. If she sits down, then this could turn into a long conversation, and I don't want that.

When I am sure that we are out of earshot of Michael in the kitchen, I take a deep breath and begin my carefully rehearsed spiel.

'I'm really sorry, but I'm afraid we are unable to continue with my son's lessons,' I say.

Petra genuinely looks surprised which is both good and bad. Good because it means that Michael kept his word and didn't tell her. Bad because it means I am the one who has to tell her.

'Oh,' Petra replies. 'Did I do something wrong?'

I feel even worse about this whole thing now that Petra has automatically assumed that she has made a mistake that has cost her her job. It might have been easier if she got defensive or argumentative, but she is being nice, which only makes me feel worse.

'No it's not that at all,' I say quickly. 'You've been great. It's just that my husband and I are going through some financial difficulties at the moment and we need to try and save some money where we can.'

I was planning on telling her that we were looking for somebody with more experience, but I have chickened out because I don't want to offend her.

'Oh, I'm sorry to hear that,' Petra says. 'I hope your jobs are okay?'

'Yeah, they are for now, but they might not be,' I lie, figuring I can't say that everything is fine now that I have gone down this route.

'Okay, well I understand,' Petra says with a sympathetic look. She feels sorry for me, which only adds to the unsettling feeling in my stomach that maybe this isn't the best thing to do. But then I think about how I will be less stressed when Sue is the one coming to our house instead of this goddess before me, so I forge on with the plan.

'Thank you. I'm sorry about this. I know you might have been counting on the money, but I hope you can find another student soon?'

'Oh yeah, don't worry about me. I'll be fine,' Petra replies, and I believe her. I doubt a woman like her will struggle to find success in this world.

'That's great. Thank you for all your hard work with Michael, and I am sure that he has learnt a lot in your short time together.'

'No problem. He's a great student and a lovely kid.'

I think about how Michael would hate being referred to as a kid and especially by someone I'm sure he fancies, but he is in the other room so he has been spared that.

I turn and head for the front door, satisfied that this has been a successful outcome and the awkwardness is now at an end. But then we reach the door, and I'm just about to open it when Petra speaks again. But this time there is no hint of the friendly and polite woman that I was speaking with a few seconds ago.

Instead, I suddenly see a whole different side of her.

'It's probably for the best anyway. Your husband is a very handsome man. I spoke with him on the driveway last week, and we got on very well. I was rather hoping to get to know him a little more. We could have had some fun together. Never mind.'

With that, Petra turns and walks away up the driveway. I'm too surprised by what she just said to call after her, and by the time I feel ready to formulate a response, she is already in her car and closing the door.

The cheeky bitch. I can't believe she just said that she fancies my husband.

I have no doubt about it now.

She needed to go.

And now she has.

34

PETRA

I can't take the smile off my face as I drive home. Catching sight of myself in the rear-view mirror, I don't look like somebody who has just lost their job. Of course, I haven't. Not really. Being a tutor isn't my profession. It's just the way I was able to extricate myself into the Lever family's lives.

I applaud Amy for her intuition. She has obviously got a bad feeling about me and decided to stop the lessons. While she can't even begin to comprehend the reality of who I am and what I am capable of, I do respect that she has at least had an inkling of trouble.

Why else would she get rid of me?

I don't believe for one minute that it has anything to do with her overhearing my conversation with Michael in which he told me about his parents' sex lives. I just agreed with him on that because I know he likes it when I do that. But in reality, I know Amy's decision is because of what could happen in that house rather than what has happened yet.

Amy sees me as a threat, which she should. I'm smarter, better looking and younger than she is. She would have known that her husband and son would become enamoured with me. I'm guessing that her jealousy of me has got the better of her. Not that anything has actually happened yet. Barring a brief chat with Nick on the driveway, I haven't even begun to get my claws into him. But I was planning on doing so, and that is still the plan. I'll just have to reconfigure it slightly. Fortunately, Michael has proven to be quite resourceful and has told me that he would like us to continue our lessons behind his mother's back. He is willing to come to my place to keep studying with me. Of course, the main goal for me is still to get back inside his house, but I already have a few ideas about how I can do that.

I feel quite excited as I drive on through the dreary suburban streets. It's a good job that I am passionate about my work because there isn't much else to inspire me around here. It's dark, it's drizzling, and every house in this two-bit town looks exactly the same as all the others.

Middle-class families, middle-aged homeowners, middle England.

I'm glad I'm not stuck here forever. I'll be out of here soon enough.

I'll be out of here as soon as I have accomplished my goal.

I must have been completely lost in my daydream because I fail to see the jogger until I almost hit him. Slamming on the brakes, I bring my car to a stop inches away from the terrified man in my headlights. His wide eyes stare at me through my windscreen, and it is clear that he didn't see me coming just as much as I didn't see him.

But this isn't just some random jogger after all.

It's Nick.

I wind my window down and poke my head outside.

'I'm sorry! You came out of nowhere!' I say, hoping that my lame excuse of an apology can make up for the fact that I nearly mowed this man down five minutes away from where his family live.

Nick seems surprised to see me but more relieved that he is still alive to see anybody at all after narrowly avoiding the collision with my front bumper. He makes his way around to my window and I see that his skin is glistening. It's a combination of the rain and the sweat from his exertion, and I like it.

He's rugged.

Active.

And out of breath.

'Thanks for stopping,' he quips as he puts his hands on his hips and sucks in mouthfuls of the cold night air.

'I figured your wife might hate me if I ran you over,' I reply with a cheeky smile.

'Yeah, she'll be glad you stopped. My kids too.'

I laugh before allowing my eyes to wander down from his face to his athletic body. I want him to see what I am doing.

I want him to know that I like what I see.

'I didn't realise how late it was,' Nick says, making a point of checking the Fitbit on his wrist. 'I guess you've just finished your lesson with Michael.'

I don't buy it for a second. I'm sure he knows exactly what time it is. I bet he has purposefully stayed out this late so he could avoid having to be there with his wife when she told me that she didn't want me to be their son's tutor anymore.

'Yep, all done. It was a good session. Shame it was my last.'

Nick looks instantly sheepish.

'I guess Amy spoke to you,' he says, and I nod. I wonder if he is going to trot out the same excuse that she used on me about how they can't afford to keep me on. But he doesn't say anything at all, and I assume it is because he already knows that any excuse is bullshit.

'It's fine, I understand,' I say, keeping my voice light. 'It's a shame though. Michael's a great kid.'

'Yeah, he is,' Nick replies, looking like the proud father for a moment which makes me like him even more.

'So I guess this is goodbye then,' I say, taking my eyes off him and returning them to the road ahead. I wonder what he will say next. I have a feeling he won't want this to be goodbye after all.

'Look, let me have a word with my wife. Maybe we can figure out the finances and keep the lessons going.'

I knew it. He doesn't want me to go at all.

This is all Amy.

'Don't worry about it. I've got other students. If you guys need to save money, then that's fine. I know that times are tough right now.'

I'm deliberately hitting on the pretence that he is short for money because I expect it will make him feel bad if I think he is struggling to provide for his family.

'No, that's not it. It's just...'

He stops speaking as if he knows that Amy would be annoyed with him if he actually told me the truth.

'Hopefully I'll see you around,' I say. 'This is a small place, after all.'

I wink at Nick then put my car into gear and drive on.

I see him in the rear-view mirror watching me leave. By the time I reach the end of the street he has turned and started jogging home. He is on his way back to his wife.

But I know that it is me who is on his mind as he goes.

35

NICK

I'm shattered. I've been out running for nearly two hours, although I have stopped and walked several times to break it up. The whole point of me being out was to avoid Petra and in particular, the awkward conversation where my wife tells her that she won't be teaching Michael anymore. But in the end, I saw Petra anyway.

She almost ran me over.

I should have been paying more attention as I crossed the road, and I was fortunate that the driver was so quick on the brakes. But I couldn't believe it when I had looked up and seen who it was behind the wheel. My son's tutor. The woman who was the reason for me being out here at this time in the first place.

I could have just carried on running, but I had stopped and spoken with Petra. I learnt that Amy had told her we can't afford to pay her for any more lessons, which is the reason my wife and I had agreed on, even if it isn't the truth. The truth is that my wife gets jealous of me around pretty women and has decided to get rid of the first one that has been around me in years. I can't blame her for that. It's my own fault.

But it's still annoying.

I'm running fast as I approach my street, but it's not because I'm feeling incredibly energetic or motivated. It's because I'm frustrated. Petra has gone, Michael has to put up with a new tutor that he definitely won't like as much and I'm left feeling like my wife still doesn't trust me. I would never hurt Amy again. I learnt my lesson after the first mistake. But she still acts as if I'm some wild animal that needs to be locked up at home away from all other women in case I can't help myself again. But nothing would have happened between the tutor and me. At most, there would have been a little harmless flirting. But it would never have led to anything. I would have made sure of that.

I see my house at the end of the street, but it's interspersed with the vision of Petra just before she drove away. That cheeky smile and wink made me feel like a man again, yet I'm on my way home now to where my wife is going to make me feel like a boy. I get that Amy is scarred from what happened, but so am I. While she might have trust issues for the rest of our marriage, she has to consider that I also have issues because of that.

Keeping me in this bubble of distrust is only making me want to break out of it even more.

I'm about fifty yards away from my house when I feel the searing pain in the right side of my abdomen. It's a stitch and it's caused by me running too fast. I'm not fit enough to be going at this speed for this long, and I'm definitely overdoing it. The stabbing pain in my side is evidence of that. But still, I refuse to stop running, going even faster now and pushing my heart rate up as high as I can get it to go before I reach my front door.

I feel alive at this moment, but I know that feeling is going to stop as soon as I step inside my house and go back to my normal routine. Work in the study. Do some housework. Chat to my wife about work.

Chat to my kids about their schoolwork. Work, work, work. I wish I could feel the way I feel now more often.

Energetic. Motivated. Alive.

I know the running is causing me to feel good in the short term, but there isn't anything I can do to keep this feeling going in the long term. Actually, there is. I know exactly what I could do to feel like this on an ongoing basis. But I can't allow myself to think about it too much. I made a promise to my wife and myself that I would never have an affair again.

Just get inside, close the door and go and give Amy a kiss on the cheek. Then stop thinking about Petra and stop thinking about what it would be like to see her again.

I've barely been home five minutes when I realise that it isn't going to be as easy as that.

THE EIGHTH LESSON

The envelopes were opened in different ways. Some of them were ripped apart enthusiastically by excited hands eager to see what the contents would reveal. Some were carefully unsealed by owners who were conscious not to damage the paperwork inside. And some were opened begrudgingly, more out of necessity rather than any real desire to find out what their fate would be. But all envelopes did get opened. Whether the pupil loved school or hated it, they still had to find out if they had passed their exams.

Some celebrated. Some cried. Some laughed. And some ripped the paper to shreds because they just didn't care anymore now that it was over. But all of them got their results. All of them got their just rewards for the amount of hard work and effort they had put into their secondary school careers.

But there was one pupil who didn't receive a letter. She wasn't present in the hall that day, nor was she visited by a postman while she sat at home and looked out on her quiet street. She had no letter to open because she had no results to receive. Her exams had been cancelled, and her future was still very much in doubt, unlike all her classmates who had just found out if their post-school plans could now go ahead.

That's because she was waiting to get the final verdict from the judge who was presiding over her case. She was waiting to find out if she would be found guilty of burning the school down and killing the teacher who had been working late inside.

GCSE results day is surely one of the most stressful days in any person's life, but it pales into comparison when put up against the possibility of prison time. The differences between an A, B, C or D are nothing compared to the difference between being able to walk around in the fresh air as a free person or being condemned to a small cell. All those fears, tears and cheers that the pupils of Sharpbell High were experiencing today were nothing compared to the emotions running through that girl as she waited for her own results day.

There was no emotion when the verdict finally came down. She didn't phone her parents to give them the news because they were sitting behind her in the dock. She didn't celebrate with her friends because they had all cut ties with her. And she didn't have the chance to look back on all the hard work and sacrifices she had made to reach this point like all the other pupils did that day. All she could do was think about how much of an injustice this was.

The eighth lesson is that nobody forgets their results day.

36

AMY

I'm still raging when I hear Nick walk through the door. Petra left ten minutes ago, and her departing comments are still ringing in my ears. Telling me that she finds my husband attractive and that the two of them could have had fun together is disgraceful.

Who the hell does she think she is?

I should have run after her. I should have kicked her off my driveway instead of letting her walk off it. I should have reminded her that beauty doesn't mean she can get away with making comments like that. But I didn't. I just watched her drive away. At least she is gone now.

My intuition was right.

She was a threat.

I can hear Nick puffing and panting in the downstairs hallway as he takes off his trainers and I'm already on my way out of the bedroom to tell him what Petra said. But I pause just before I reach the stairs.

My paranoia has kicked in again.

Should I tell Nick that Petra likes him? How will that make him feel? What if he likes her too? I know it's stupid and I know he will take my side, but I find myself not saying the words that I had been waiting to say when he got back. Of course, he will tell me that she shouldn't have said those things and he will probably be as disgusted as I am. But how will I know what he is really thinking? How do I know that he won't secretly be thrilled to find out that the Swedish tutor found him attractive?

'You okay?'

I look down and see Nick staring up at me from the bottom of the stairs. His cheeks are flushed, and he looks either incredibly sweaty or incredibly wet from the rain, but he also looks concerned. He is probably wondering why I am standing at the top of the stairs and looking down at him without saying anything.

'Yeah, fine!' I reply quickly. 'Good run?'

'It was alright,' Nick says, pulling off his waterproof jacket. 'Managed to go further than I expected.'

'You were gone ages,' I say, because only now do I realise how long he has actually been gone.

'Yeah sorry, I got carried away,' he tells me, but I know he is lying.

'You mean you didn't want to be here when I told Petra that the lessons were ending?'

He looks up at me with that uncomfortable look he wears so well.

'How did she take it?' he asks me, and I decide there and then not to tell him everything that was said between us.

'She was fine. She understood.'

Nick nods.

'I'm going to jump in the shower. Are the kids in their rooms?'

'Where else would they be?'

He smiles as he heads up the stairs towards me, and I step back to make room for him on the landing. But instead of moving past me and heading into the bathroom, he stops and puts his hand around my waist.

Then he pulls me in for a kiss.

I'm surprised, but our lips are touching before I can get any words out. When they finally part, I feel almost as flushed as he is.

He winks at me then heads for the bathroom before closing the door and turning the lock. I stand there for a moment thinking about what just happened. The kiss was nice, but something is troubling me. Nick never does things like that. Spontaneous bursts of affection aren't really his thing. There was only one other time that I can remember him just grabbing me and kissing me passionately out of the blue.

It was just before I found out about him and Tina.

My husband is only passionate when he has someone else on his mind. That time it was his co-worker. But this time who could it be? It can't be Petra. He wasn't here when she left. He hasn't seen her tonight. And he knows he is never going to see her again.

But that doesn't mean he isn't thinking about her.

What did they really talk about on the driveway that night? What was Petra really saying when she told me that she could have had some fun with Nick? Was she just winding me up because I had let her go? Was she wistfully thinking out loud about not being able to see the man she fancied anymore? Or was she lulling me into a false sense of security and is really planning on seeing Nick again?

There are so many questions bouncing around in my head right now. The counsellor I saw after Nick's affair warned me about this. She told me that staying with him might mean that I am always on edge whenever another woman comes into our lives. I hadn't believed it. I thought I was stronger than that. That's why I was happy to give Petra the job. But now I know the truth. I still feel just as weak and helpless as I did when I found out about the affair with Tina.

As I listen to Nick whistling in the shower on the other side of the bathroom door, I still feel like something is going to go wrong with my carefully constructed life.

Most of all, I feel afraid.

37

MICHAEL

My new tutor is not as interesting as my old one. Sue is a nice enough woman, and she certainly knows her stuff when it comes to GCSE Maths, but I don't exactly have the same connection with her as I had with Petra. She doesn't ask me any personal questions for one thing. In fact, she has made no effort at all to try and get to know me better. All she is interested in is asking me the questions in the textbooks. That is exactly what she has been hired to do, but I can't help it if I'm not as engaged with her as I was with my old tutor. I can't help it if she isn't quite the same. And I can't help it if I miss Petra.

But it's not for long.

I am seeing her tomorrow night, and I can't wait.

As far as my parents know, these lessons with Sue are the only extra tutoring I am getting now. But I am secretly going to

Petra's flat tomorrow, and I am going to continue the lessons we started together before Mum and Dad rudely interrupted them. I can't tell anybody about my plan, not even my friends at school. While I know they will be devastatingly jealous that I am going to be alone with Petra at her place, I cannot risk the news leaking out and getting back to my parents. I have to keep this quiet.

I have to sacrifice a short-term gain for what will hopefully be a long term one.

I am going to make a move on Petra. I'm not exactly sure when and I'm not exactly sure how but I am going to do it. At some point in one of our lessons, when I am sure that she is going to be receptive, I will move in for a kiss. She could turn me down, but I have to try. And I have a feeling that my chances of success are greater now that we will be at her place away from the watchful eyes of my parents.

I can't let the fact that my success rate with the opposite sex has been limited thus far in my life. This is different. Petra isn't some teenager who doesn't know what she wants. She is an adult, and she is so much better than any of the girls at my school. I feel sorry for my friends because they are only around girls our age. But I'm lucky. I get to be around a real woman.

But it's going to cost me.

'It's worth more than that!' I say to the bearded man behind the counter. 'It's not even been out a year!'

'I don't care. I can't sell it for more than that so I can't pay more than that for it, can I?' the man replies with a weary tone to his voice that suggests that he wants to be doing something more with his life than working in a video game store on the high street.

'You can give me thirty for it, surely?' I suggest hopefully, but the shake of the head I get in response is confirmation that I am not going to get more than twenty pounds for trading in this old game.

I let out a deep breath and slide the case containing the old football game across the counter. The man slides me a twenty-pound note in return, and I walk out of the shop, consoling myself with the knowledge that I can at least afford my next couple of lessons with Petra now. I don't mind selling off an old video game to raise the last bit of money I needed to fund my extra-curricular activities with the Swedish woman. I hardly ever play that particular game anyway, but neither does anybody else which explains why that guy was unwilling to pay me any more for it. But I have the cash to give to Petra tonight and that is all that matters for now. I can think about how I am going to get the rest of the money for the following weeks later. I can do some extra chores at home if I have to. It's not as if Mum and Dad will ever find out what I am spending my pocket money on.

But an exciting thought occurs to me as I prepare to cross the high street and head on towards the bus stop that will take me back home. Maybe I won't have to keep paying to see Petra. Maybe she will want to see me just because she likes me and not because I am a paying customer. That all hinges on the kiss going well. If I nail it, then it could happen. Then I won't have to give her any more money, and she won't have to teach me any more Maths.

We could spend our time together doing more interesting things instead...

The sound of the car horn to my left almost makes me jump out of my skin, and I turn around to see the angry motorist through the windscreen of the white van that almost hit me.

'It's a green light!' the animated man behind the wheel shouts at me through his open window, and I hold up my hand in apology before scuttling quickly across the road and making it back to the safety of the pavement.

That was my fault. I wasn't paying attention to the traffic lights. I wasn't concentrating on what I was doing at the time. That's because I'm thinking about Petra. I can't help it. She is all I think about. I wonder if this is just a crush or if it is something more. I don't ever remember feeling this strongly about someone before. I'm usually just thinking about football. But now I'm only thinking about her.

I reach the bus stop and watch the bus trundling down the road towards me, and I can't help but feel happy. It's only a few hours now until I get to see Petra again. And this time Mum and Dad won't be listening to our conversations on the other side of the door.

They won’t be anywhere near us.

38

PETRA

'Welcome to my humble abode,' I say to the teenage boy on my doorstep.

I step aside and allow him into my flat, closing the door quickly so that nobody on my floor can see him coming in. It's not that I have anything to hide but rather that I don't want my neighbours wondering why I am having youngsters visiting me at my flat. I don't want them to think about anything when it comes to me. I want to be unremarkable, unnoticeable and entirely forgettable. That makes it easier when I eventually leave this place and move onto the next.

'Nice flat,' Michael says, and I think he is being sarcastic until I realise that he probably means it because to him, this is a nice flat. It's somewhere to call my own, and for a sixteen-year-old who lives under his parents' roof, that is the ultimate dream.

'Thanks. It's not the biggest, but I like it,' I say, and I'm not lying. The flat is nothing special, just a one-bedroom place with a tiny bathroom and the kitchen and living area combined into one room. But it is fine for what I need it for, which is just a place to base myself for the time being. I will be able to afford somewhere much bigger than this soon, but there is no point spending more than I need to right now. One day I will settle down and treat myself to the kind of home that all my hard work deserves.

'Can I get you a drink?' I ask Michael as he takes off his hoodie and drapes it over the edge of the sofa.

'Have you got any beer?' he asks cheekily, and I know that he is joking, but I'm feeling like a good host.

'Is Peroni okay?'

Michael seems surprised by my answer. He's too young to be drinking, but I'm not his mum. He can do whatever he wants when he is under my roof.

'Errr yeah, sure.'

I smile and head for the fridge, amused by how grown-up Michael just tried to make himself seem with his answer. I wonder how many beers he has had in his life. Other than a couple in the park with his friends or maybe one at Christmas with his dad, I doubt he has much experience when it comes to alcohol intake. But he is more than welcome to have one although the fact that I have bought them in for his dad rather than him means I will only be offering him the one.

Popping the cap on the bottle, I deliver Michael his beer before returning to the kitchen counter where I pour myself my second glass of wine of the evening. Glancing up as I work, I see Michael standing awkwardly by the sofa, clearly too polite to sit down and make himself at home even though he surely wants to. I could tell him to sit, but I like the fact that he is uncomfortable. It's a different kind of awkwardness to the one he displayed when I was in his own home. He is still nervous around me but for different reasons now.

Picking up my glass, I leave the kitchen and walk into the living area where my pupil awaits. That's the one good thing about having a small flat. I don't have to take more than a couple of steps to get to the next room.

'Cheers,' I say, holding out my glass towards him.

'Oh yeah, cheers,' Michael replies, and he clinks his beer against my wine except he does it a little too hard and the alcohol starts foaming out of the top of the bottle.

'Shit, sorry!' he says, putting his hand over the top of the bottle, which he probably thinks is the right thing to do but only demonstrates to me how inexperienced he is with drinking. Anybody who has had this happen to them before would know that it is better to put the top of the bottle in your mouth to collect the frothing beer that way instead of just putting your hand over it and letting it drip all over the place.

'Don't worry about it. It's not the first drink to be spilt here, and I'm sure it won't be the last.'

I grab the tea towel from the kitchen counter and hand it to Michael, who quickly cleans up his mess. I wait until he is certain that he has got it all before taking back the towel and tossing it back into the kitchen. Finally, I think we are ready to begin.

'Shall we get started then?' I suggest.

'Yeah, can do,' Michael replies, and I'm positive I detect a bit of disappointment in his face as he says it. He was probably hoping that we would spend the first half an hour drinking and chatting about ourselves instead of revising, but it can't all be fun and games.

Which reminds me...

'Have you got the money?' I ask as I place my wine glass down on a coaster and take a seat on the sofa.

'Yeah, sure,' Michael replies and he fishes inside his pockets for a moment before producing a couple of scrunched up twenty-pound notes.

'Thanks,' I say as he hands them to me, and I place them down beside my glass. Then I pat the empty sofa seat beside me.

'Come on, don't be shy,' I say to my extremely shy student.

Michael finally allows himself to relax enough to take a seat and we are ready to get going.

I take out the Maths textbook from beneath the coffee table and turn it to page sixty. Statistics. How exciting. But Michael is paying me to teach him, so I need to give him his money's worth. He's already got a free beer out of me. What more does he want?

It isn't long until I get my answer.

39

AMY

It's not often I get the house to myself, but that is a luxury I am enjoying right now. Nick is out on another run, Michael is round at Nev's house, and Bella is doing a sponsored sleepover with her classmates in the school hall. That means my home is filled with the sweet sounds of silence, or at least it will be until I turn on the television and settle down with a glass of red wine.

I'm feeling much better about things than I was last week. I think I had just built the whole thing with Petra up into a massive problem in my mind when there wasn't anything to worry about. My paranoia over what Nick has done to me in the past had reared its ugly head again. But now the dust has settled, and I'm able to think more clearly. Petra said those things to me because she was annoyed that I had let her go. I can see that now. She didn't mean anything by it; she was just trying to get back at me after I told her we were not going to be paying her anymore. Likewise, Nick being spontaneously intimate with me at the top of the stairs after his run wasn't because he was thinking about her or any other women for that matter, it was because he was full of adrenaline after his jog that evening. And any other feelings of jealously or anxiety are just down to my issues with what happened with my husband and that other woman all those years ago and nothing to do with anything that is happening right now.

The large gulp of wine that I have just taken has already worked wonders, and I feel myself relaxing. It helps that the house is peaceful and it helps that it is almost the weekend again. I'm looking forward to this particular one because I have plans to see three of my friends in Birmingham on Saturday. We are going to have an afternoon of retail therapy before cocktails and cheeseboards, and I cannot wait. It's just what I need. A day out of the house. A day away from any responsibility. And a day away from my usual bouts of paranoia.

I've been so stressed recently about Michael's exams, Bella's bullying and the fact that my husband may or may not fancy the Swedish tutor that I haven't taken any time to focus on myself. But that is going to change this weekend.

This weekend is about having some fun.

I have just started to lose myself in one of my favourite reality shows when I hear the ping from my phone on the coffee table. Picking up my mobile while keeping my eyes on the TV screen, I am in no rush to check the message until the scene has finished. It won't be anything important anyway. Probably just one of my friends talking about how they can't wait to get drunk on Saturday. But then I look down at the notification and see that it isn't a message from my friends. Nor is it a message from anyone in my family. I have no idea who has sent this because I don't recognise the number. There aren't any words that could help me figure out who it's from either. There's just a photo attachment which I can't make out until I open the full message.

Unlocking my phone, I wait a couple of seconds to allow the photo to open up on my screen. When it does, the glass of wine falls out of my hand and spills onto the carpet. But I'm so shocked that I don't even care about what I've just done. All I care about is the person in the photo looking back at me through the screen. It's a face that I haven't seen in many years, and it is a person that I have done my best to forget about. But just like my husband's infidelity, it seems there are other things that will never leave me alone.

I hear the front door opening. Nick must be back from his latest jog. He knows something is wrong when he sees my face.

He gets confirmation of that fact when I show him the photo.

40

MICHAEL

I'm glad I've been out of the house all night. Mum and Dad seemed in a bad mood when I got in, so I just left them to it and came straight up to my room. If they knew where I had really been then their mood would be even worse. They think I've been at Nev's house playing FIFA, but I've really been at Petra's flat drinking beer and listening to her tell me about her childhood. We did do a little revision but not enough to make a dent in my upcoming exams. But I don't care. I'm not paying her to teach me how to get better grades. I'm paying her so that I can keep seeing her.

So far, it is working.

Mum and Dad have no idea, and that is the way I will keep it. I wish I could tell them how happy my tutor makes me, but I can't. They won't understand. They will just think it is some childish crush. But it's more than that. I really like Petra. I mean, really, really like her.

I have a feeling it might even be more than that.

I think I might love her.

I have gotten over the fact that she is hot. Having gotten to know her more over the last few weeks, I now know that there is a smart, creative and funny person beneath the beautiful looks. My friends would tease me if I told them that I liked her as much for her brains as for her beauty, which is exactly why I won't be telling them that. I won't be telling anybody how I really feel.

Except her. I have to tell her.

But when?

I don't want to do it when the time isn't right and push her away. I have to wait for the perfect moment. It will come along soon, I'm sure of it. It just didn't come tonight.

I've spent the last two hours sitting on the sofa in Petra's flat wishing that I could lean forward and kiss her, but the moment never came. Not that it was a bad night. Not by any means. The beer was great, as was the fact that I got to sit so close to her and hear her mesmerising accent. But best of all, I have learnt even more about her background.

She told me about what it was like going to school in Stockholm. She told me about how she struggled to learn English for the longest time until suddenly it clicked with her. That was when she fell in love with the language. She told me about how she wasn't a particularly good student because she couldn't wait to leave the textbooks behind and get out into the real world. And she told me that she had no idea what she wanted to do with her life when she was older, but she knew things would work out well in the end.

Essentially, she told me that she was just like me when she was my age.

I'm not getting carried away when I say that we have so much in common. The only real difference I can see between us is with our ages, which is an obstacle but not an insurmountable one. I like that word insurmountable. I like it because Petra told me it was one of her favourite words in the English language once she had finally figured out how to say it. She told me she likes it because of what it means. She likes the fact that it is used to describe a problem that seems too big to overcome because, in her mind, there is no problem that is too big to overcome. That is why she seeks out challenges and problems that seem insurmountable, just so she can crush them and leave them lying in her wake.

She told me that her moving to England had seemed like an insurmountable dream when she had first had it many years ago. Her parents were dead against it, she had no money to her name, and she didn't know a single person in this country who could have helped her when she got here. Yet still, she decided to give it a go, believing that she would be able to overcome all the hurdles of her family's grievances, her lack of money and her lack of any friendship here to start a new life in a new country where she longed to be.

I find so much inspiration in that, and my only regret is that I hadn't told her so. I should have said it instead of just sitting there and listening to her whilst trying to look cool with my beer bottle in my hand. I should have been genuine with her instead of trying to give off this air of maturity and composure that I always find myself putting on whenever I am around her. But yet again, I found myself not saying much at all, too enamoured by the woman in front of me and too preoccupied with worrying about making myself look more grown-up than I actually am.

But I need to change my tactics. I won't get Petra by being fake. I need to be genuine. I need to be myself. I need to show her the real me so she can see past all the bravado and the cocky false confidence and learn about who I really am.

That is the only way to find out if she likes me as much as I like her.

A loud burp escapes from my mouth and catches me by surprise as I lie on my bed and stare up at the ceiling. I smile at the sound of it because I know what caused it. It was that beer that I had at Petra's. The beer that she offered me because she sees me as a grown up and not a child like Mum and Dad or my schoolteachers do. It was the beer that tasted so sweet as I sipped it whilst listening to my tutor talk. It was also the beer that I spilt on her carpet after it fizzed up but never mind about that. That was just a small blip in what was an otherwise successful evening.

I had a great time tonight. I enjoyed all of it, even the little part of the night when we actually did some revision. And I enjoy the feeling that is buzzing through my body right now.

There's no doubt about it.

I love being in love.

THE NINTH LESSON

There were a few people in the town who didn't believe it, but they were in the minority. They also were not in any position to change the situation. The girl who had been found guilty of burning down the school and inadvertently killing the teacher had been sentenced to five years in prison, which was not enough for the victim's family but too much for the innocent person who would be serving it.

That first night inside was the worst. The girl cried herself to sleep in her bed, trying to come to terms with the fact that she had done nothing wrong yet found herself in a place like that, alongside real criminals. She had hoped that her tender age might have led to a more lenient sentence and certainly one that would be carried out in a minimum-security prison, but it was not to be. The judge could have given her more years, but five was still enough. And the prison she was placed in to serve out that sentence was no holiday camp.

She made no friends there, mainly because she didn't speak to anybody but also because she didn't want to. The other inmates weren't like her.

They actually belonged in a place like this.

Fights broke out almost daily. One woman had her hair pulled from her scalp during an argument with another inmate. And one unlucky prisoner got beaten up so badly that she suffered a punctured lung and died on the way to the ward.

Despite the hell that she found herself in, the young woman was hopeful that justice would be done and the truth would come out, overturning the sentence and seeing her released back into society. But the problem was that nobody seemed to know the truth about the fire, especially not the woman who had been found guilty. That made it impossible for the police to reopen the case and keep digging for the real answers. Of course, somebody knew the truth. The person who started that fire knew what they had done and what they had gotten away with. But that wasn't much help to the inmate serving a sentence for someone else's crimes.

She was the one trapped inside.

It was precisely two years and nine days into the injustice of a sentence when the innocent prisoner was strangled in her bed by a deranged inmate who had secretly stopped taking her medication for schizophrenia. The crazed woman had suffered a manic episode and believed that the eighteen-year-old woman in that cell was the devil. It was too late to tell her that she was wrong. That poor innocent woman was no devil, but she was now dead.

The ninth lesson is that the line between good and evil becomes blurred in a place that holds both.

41

AMY

The last couple of days have gone by in a blur. Nick and I have been getting on each other's nerves, Michael has been sneaking out to go to his friend's house instead of revising, and Bella has told me that the bullying has started again. But that's not even the worst of it.

That photo is still on my phone, and I have no idea who sent it to me.

The photo is the reason why my husband and I have been clashing this week. He keeps trying to make me believe that it is no big deal and is telling me not to worry about it whereas I think it is a harbinger of doom and could spell the end for our family. Maybe neither of us are right.

It has to mean something or why would I have been sent it? But maybe it isn't as bad as I think. It could just be somebody playing a prank. Perhaps other people around town have received the photo too. It's coming up to the twenty-fifth anniversary of the fire. The story is starting to crop up in the local news again because of that. It probably is just a prank.

So why do I feel so worried?

I'm on the train to Birmingham with my friends and spirits are high at our table which is covered in small cans of Gin & Tonic and big packets of crisps. I seem to be the only one struggling to get into the party mood. I've been looking forward to this day for weeks, but that was before I got the message on my phone.

That put a dampener on everything.

'What do you say, Amy?'

I look up from the table and notice that my friends are all looking at me. There's Sarah and Diane opposite, who I have known since primary school, and Michelle in the seat beside me, who entered our group in secondary. We are the loyal schoolfriends that kept in touch, which I like because it means that I know everything about them and they know everything about me.

Well, almost everything.

'Sorry, I missed that,' I say, reaching for another snack.

'Dinner tonight. Chinese or Thai?' Sarah asks, and I should have known it was about food because that is her favourite topic of conversation these days. She's already spent the first part of this train journey telling us about how her latest diet isn't working. I'm guessing she has just decided to abandon it altogether if her suggestions for our evening meal are anything to go by.

'Either is good with me,' I say because it is. I like all foods. I'm not fussy. And I have much more important things to think about right now.

'What about Indian?' Diane suddenly suggests, and that is the catalyst for another five minutes of them discussing tasty options. I zone out again and go back to the train of thought that has been running through my mind ever since I received that photo on my phone. I still don't know who sent it because I don't recognise the number. But there is a way to try and find out.

I could call it and see if anybody answers.

I’ve been scared to do it so far, but I have a feeling I might have a little more confidence if I keep drinking at the pace that the girls have decided to go at today. I’m already on my second G & T, and it’s not even lunchtime. A few more and I might just pluck up the courage to press the little green phone symbol beside the mystery number. They might not answer, but I have to try. That is the only way I am going to find out who sent that photo.

I did text them yesterday with a simple message: ***Who is this?***

But I got no response.

I haven’t told Nick that I am trying to engage with this person. He thinks I have already deleted the message and moved on. But I’m not like him. I can’t just compartmentalise my thoughts into neat little boxes as if I’m tidying up in the spare bedroom. I dwell on things. I obsess over them. And I worry myself into a frenzy over them. That is why I feel so drained now on what should have been a fun day for me. I’m out of the house. I’m away from my responsibilities for the day. I'm with my best friends. I should be laughing, snacking and chatting without a care in the world, just like they are. Instead, my thoughts are zooming around my head as fast as the countryside is zooming past this train window.

I think about my family to try and calm myself down. Bella is at her regular Saturday morning dance class, which I am glad about because it will help take her mind off the teasing at school, which I now need to speak to the teacher about again on Monday. Michael has his Under-17's football match at the local Boys & Girls Club to keep him busy before he has to go home and do some revising because that's what I've told him he needs to do. And Nick will be around the house and on standby for picking up the kids from their various activities and getting them home, as well as cooking them dinner and generally keeping them out of mischief until I arrive back later tonight.

It's a simple Saturday. A standard Saturday. A nothing special about it Saturday.

So why does it feel like today is going to be a bad day?

42

PETRA

I know that Amy is out of the house. Michael and Bella are too. That leaves Nick home alone.

It's about time he had some company.

I stride down the driveway past the spot where Nick and I had our brief chat a few weeks ago and reach the front door. I'm about to knock but take a couple of seconds beforehand to fiddle with my hair. I want to look perfect when he opens the door to me.

I want to take his breath away.

Knock knock knock. Three simple taps on the door with my delicate hand will be all it takes to get Nick scurrying out of his study and on his way towards me. I presume he is in his study. I can't know for sure, but it seems like he is always in there. Unless he is out for another run.

Oh god, what if he isn't home? Then my plan will be ruined. That would be so…

The door swings open and Nick is suddenly standing before me.

'Hey!' I say, flashing him my biggest smile.

He looks momentarily confused, which he should be because there is no reason why I should be here. Or at least I haven't given him one yet.

'Hello?' he says, but it's more of a question than a greeting.

'Sorry to bother you but I've just realised I've left one of my textbooks here,' I say, keeping my voice as light and breezy as the flowery dress that I am wearing. I'm not at all dressed for the weather today, which is grey and chilly, but I'm trying to look sexy, not sensible.

'Oh. Okay,' Nick replies, doing a good job of keeping his eyes on my face and not my dress, even though he must be tempted to look down.

'I'm not sure where but it must be here because I've looked everywhere else. I must have left it here after my last lesson with Michael.'

'I see,' Nick says, and he looks back over his shoulder into the house as if that will confirm to him if I am telling the truth or not.

'Could you just check? It's just it's quite an expensive book and I need it for my other students.'

'Sure, let's have a look. Like you say, it must be here somewhere. It has probably got mixed up with Michael's books.'

Nick steps back into the house but leaves the door open, and I take that as my sign to go inside too. I close the door behind myself, and without the sounds of the street outside it suddenly feels very, very quiet in here.

'Is it just you?' I ask as if I have no idea that the rest of his family are out.

'Yeah, the kids have got their activities, and Amy's on a girl's day out in Birmingham,' Nick replies as he walks towards the kitchen.

'Oh, I'm sorry to interrupt your peace and quiet,' I lie.

'Don't worry about it. I wasn't doing much anyway.'

We've walked into the kitchen and I can tell that Amy is out because the counters are full of dirty bowls, spoons and plates from what I imagine was a typically chaotic breakfast time.

'I know some of Michael's books are down here,' Nick says, walking over to the shelf near the kitchen table. 'Hopefully it's with these.'

He picks up the stack of revision textbooks from the shelf and starts going through them, and I know I should help, but I'm too busy looking at all the cookbooks that are also nearby.

'Wow, I guess Amy is quite the chef,' I say, picking up a chunky book full of traditional dessert recipes.

'Yeah, she's pretty handy in the kitchen,' Nick replies. 'Plays havoc with my waistline though.'

'Doesn't look like it,' I reply quickly, making sure that he sees me checking out his torso.

'Erm. So is it any of these?' he asks, thrusting the revision books in my direction to disguise his awkwardness at the compliment I just gave him.

I make a point of looking through them all carefully, even though I already know that the textbook won't be here. Why would it be? It's under my coffee table in my flat.

'No, I can't see it,' I reply, feigning disappointment. 'Is there anywhere else he might have put it by mistake?'

'The only other place would be his bedroom,' Nick says, and I smile because that's exactly what I was hoping he would suggest. 'I'll just go and check.'

Nick heads for the door as I place the books back on the shelf, and I wait until I hear his footsteps on the stairs before I follow him. I don't want him to know that I have followed him up there until it is too late.

I can hear him rummaging around in the upstairs bedroom as I climb the stairs, and I see the open doorway which must lead to Michael's room when I reach the landing. Walking in confidently, I find Nick on his hands and knees, pulling several textbooks out from under his son's bed.

'So this is what a teenage boy's bedroom looks like,' I say from my position by the doorway.

Nick bangs his head on the edge of the bed as he looks up, and he is clearly surprised to see that I have joined him upstairs.

'Here, let me help you,' I say, crouching down so that I am at the same height as the man beside the bed.

The floor is littered with football magazines, video game boxes and discarded items of clothing but I'm able to find a small slice of carpet to fit myself onto beside Nick, which means we are now very close together.

The man of the house is uncomfortable, but he does his best to keep to the task at hand.

'Is it any of these?' he asks, referencing the numerous textbooks that he has pulled out from under the bed.

He clearly doesn't have a clue what he is looking for because some of these books refer to school years that Michael has long since left behind, but I don't tell him that.

'Hmmm, I can't see it,' I say. 'But then it's hard to see anything in here.'

Nick laughs at my joke, and I'm glad because I need to keep it light. I need to keep his mind off the fact that his wife would kill him if she knew that he was in this house alone with me, never mind his son for letting me into his bedroom.

'Yeah, it is a bit of a tip. But then so was my room at his age,' Nick says.

I keep my eyes on the books on the floor, but I can feel him checking me out in my peripheral vision. It's time to go in for the kill.

'I have a confession to make,' I say, turning to look at him so that our faces are even closer now.

'What?' Nick asks, his eyes wandering down to my perfect red lips.

'There is no textbook. I lied about leaving it here. I knew you would be home alone today. That's why I'm here. I wanted to see you.'

Nick looks stunned by my confession, but I'm telling him the truth. I make sure I keep looking at his lips too to let him know how serious I am.

'How did you know I'd be alone?'

'Michael told me. We've been texting.'

'Why have you been texting?'

'Because I'm still teaching him. He comes to my flat. I guess he didn't want to stop seeing me. Just like I don't want to stop seeing you.'

I move my face closer towards him, inviting him to close the last little distance between us and initiate our first ever kiss. And I have a feeling he is going to do it too.

He is going to do it right up until we hear the front door open downstairs.

43

MICHAEL

'Dad, I'm home!' I call out into the quiet house as I close the front door behind me.

I dump my rucksack at the bottom of the stairs and kick off my trainers, annoyed that my football game got cancelled at the last minute but trying to look on the bright side. I can chill out and play FIFA all morning now instead.

I get no response from Dad and assume he hasn't heard me because he is locked away in the study again. I'm tempted to go up to my bedroom and start playing my game, but I had better make sure he knows that I am home or he will still be thinking that he needs to go and pick me up at lunchtime.

'Dad!'

Still no reply. He's so annoying. I bet he's got his headphones in on his laptop again. He says he is working, but I know he does it so that he doesn't have to listen to all the other things going on in the house. Mum's nagging. Bella's singing. And me trying to get his attention. But he's alone now so he shouldn't be trying to drown out the noise.

So why isn't he answering me?

'Michael?'

I turn around and see my dad standing on the staircase. He looks surprised to see me, which he should be because I shouldn't be home yet.

'There you are,' I say, rolling my eyes. 'I've been calling you.'

'What are you doing back?' he asks and I notice him glancing back up the stairs as he speaks.

'The game got cancelled. The other team didn't have enough players. Idiots. I got a lift back off Nev's mum.'

'You should have called me. I would have come and got you.'

'It's fine, I'm back now,' I say, reaching the bottom of the staircase. 'I'm gonna go play some Fifa before revising.'

I have no intention of revising, but I better say I do otherwise I won't get to play my game beforehand.

'Wait,' Dad says and he rushes down towards me, blocking my path to go up.

'What?' I ask, getting annoyed. I wish he had been out too. Then I would have had the house to myself, and I would have been playing FIFA already.

'You can't go up there.'

'Why not?'

'Because I'm planning a surprise and I don't want you to see it.'

'What surprise?'

I look past him up the stairs, but I can't see anything from down here.

'It's for after your exams. For all the hard work you are doing. But you can't go up there, or you'll see it.'

A present for after my exams? I like the sound of that.

'What is it?' I ask, even though Dad obviously won't tell me.

'It's a surprise. But I need to put it away. Can you go out in the back garden for five minutes while I move it?'

'Why can't I just stay down here?'

'Because I need to bring it down. Just do it, please.'

I'm not sure why Dad is so flustered about the whole thing, but then I figure it must be because Mum has told him to make sure that I don't find out about it until my exams are finished. She wouldn't want me to be distracted.

I can't believe they have got me a present. I actually feel a little bad for not doing more revision now.

'Okay, I'll go in the back garden. But hurry up, it looks like it's going to rain.'

I put my trainers on and head for the back door in the kitchen, annoyed at the temporary delay to getting on my games console but also excited about what this surprise present could be. They have already told me about the tickets to the E-sports festival in London if I keep having my lessons with Sue, but this must be something else.

Stepping outside, I pull the back door closed behind me and look up at the gloomy sky. It is definitely going to rain. Maybe it's a good thing the game got cancelled. I was looking forward to playing football, but it looks more like a day for playing it online in my bedroom rather than outside on a real pitch.

I wander down to the shed at the bottom of the garden and peep through the small window on the side, but I can't make out anything within as it's too dark in there. But I know that there's nothing exciting inside: just a lawnmower, a rusted barbeque and a couple of old deckchairs. Turning back to the house, I walk across the grass and wonder if enough time has passed for Dad to hide my present away and let me come back inside again.

I can feel the first few drops of rain beginning to land on my skin, and I need to get back inside sooner rather than later if I don't want to get drenched. I decide to give it one more minute. He should have finished by then. Too bad if not. If I catch a glimpse of the present, then so be it.

To pass the time, I take out my mobile phone and look at my messages. There's already a new one from Nev even though I have literally just said goodbye to him five minutes ago when his mum dropped me off. He's sent me a football meme, and it's a funny one, but I'll reply to him later. Going down through my messages, I notice the last one I sent to Petra. I had thanked her for the lesson we had the other day, but she didn't reply. No biggie. As long as we are still on for the next one, then I don't care.

Maybe I should make sure that we are.

I type out a message to her asking her if we are definitely still on for the secretive study session on Wednesday and press send. I know she might not text me back for a while. It is Saturday after all. She must be busy. I wonder what she is up to. I try not to let myself imagine her out on a date with some other guy right now.

I wait for the tick to appear on the message to tell me that it has been delivered to Petra's phone. After a couple of seconds, I see it.

I also hear the ringtone from another mobile phone at the exact same time.

That's weird. What are the odds of sending a message and hearing somebody receive one nearby at the exact same moment?

The noise sounded like it came from the front of the house. I walk down the side and see the gate that leads to the driveway. Mum and Dad always used to make sure it was closed when we were small, but they don't care as much now that we are older, which is why it is currently wide open.

I walk through it, and that's when I hear the sound of the front door closing.

I wish I'd stopped there. I wish I hadn't looked around the corner onto the driveway. Then I wouldn't have seen who was leaving. But I did.

I looked, and I saw.

I saw Petra rushing away from my house.

44

PETRA

That was close. I can't believe Michael came home. How annoying. Nick and I had just been about to kiss. I could have been in his bed right now. Instead, I'm out here in the rain trying to get back to my car before I get soaked.

I get behind the wheel and slam the door shut before taking out my mobile phone. I heard a new message come through just as I was leaving Nick's house and I want to check it before I drive. I also want to take a minute to chill. That was a stressful time trying to get downstairs and out of the house without Michael seeing me. I need to get my heart rate down before I start the engine and drive home.

I take out my phone and check the notification on the screen. But it doesn't make my heart rate go down. It does the opposite.

The message is from Michael.

Oh god, did he see me?

I look up at his house through my windscreen from where I am parked down the street, but I can't see any sign of him or anybody else looking back at me. He can't have seen me. Nick told me that Michael was in the back garden. I left via the front. There's no way he could have spotted me.

Letting out a deep breath, I open the message to see what Michael has sent. But it's just a message asking me if we are still on for our session on Wednesday. There's nothing about him seeing me today. He's not asking me what I was doing at his house with his dad while everybody else was out.

I got away with it.

Phew.

I put my phone on the car seat and turn the key in the engine. I'll wait until I get back home before I reply to the message. I'm sure Michael is checking his mobile eagerly to see if I have responded to him, but I'll make him wait. He's just spoilt my morning. It's the least he deserves.

But no sooner have I started to drive then I am forced to pull over again. Somebody is calling me, and I can't ignore this like I have just ignored Michael's message. This person demands my attention straight away.

'What do you think you are doing?' asks the person on the other end of the line, and I don't really have an answer for her. I just stay quiet and look through my car window at the house I just had to sneak out of.

I guess I did get spotted by somebody after all.

45

NICK

That was too close. What the hell was I thinking allowing her into my home when everybody else was out? I should know better than that.

I do know better than that.

I almost fucked things up for myself all over again. Michael could have seen her. He would have told his mum. Amy would have thought the worst.

She would have thought I was cheating again.

But I'm not. I haven't done anything wrong. Petra just turned up unannounced. She told me she had left a textbook behind, and I had believed her. Why wouldn't I? It was a perfectly legitimate thing to say. She could have easily left it behind after one of her lessons with Michael. How was I to know that she had an ulterior motive?

How was I to know that she was going to try and kiss me in my son's bedroom?

I managed to get her out of the house before my son saw her. It was plain bad luck that his football match was cancelled, but then maybe it was for the best. God only knows what would have happened if he hadn't walked through the front door at that exact moment.

Would we have kissed? Would we have done more? Would we now be lying in my marital bed together while my wife is out with friends in the city?

I'm glad I don't have to know the answers to those questions because we were interrupted before it could get that far. As it stands, I am still a good husband, and I intend to keep it that way. I haven't done anything wrong. Petra came onto me. She told me she liked me. I didn't say anything back. I didn't reciprocate any of it.

But maybe I didn't have to. Maybe my silence was her answer. Maybe my eyes on her lips told her all she needed to know about how I felt too. Maybe it was inevitable that we would have kissed if my son hadn't come home at the most critical of moments.

That's not even the craziest part of this whole situation though. That part is reserved for the fact that Petra has told me that Michael is still seeing her. She told me just before he came home. Apparently, he is going to her flat for study sessions. He has even been paying her with his own pocket money which explains why he has been so keen to do some extra housework lately. Not only that, but he is texting her. My sixteen-year-old son is secretly texting a twenty-eight-year-old woman. There's no way he is doing it because he wants the extra revision sessions. He is doing it because he wants her. But she is too old for him. She is an adult.

And she likes me instead.

I can't deny it. I feel excited to have been told that I am wanted by a younger woman. How could that not make me feel good? I know I can't do anything about it, but still, I can't disregard the confidence boost it has given me. But I'm married. Nothing can happen there.

My single days are long gone.

Then again, I hardly experienced them. Amy and I got together when we were sixteen. I didn't get to play the field. I was married before I knew it. Maybe the affair with Tina was inevitable. Maybe it was me trying to experience some of what I missed out on by settling down so young. Maybe it is also why I can't stop feeling the urge to see Petra again even though I know it will lead to breaking Amy's heart all over again.

But she doesn't have to find out. Nobody does. I could get away with it. I learnt my lesson from the last affair. I can avoid making the same mistakes. I can avoid Amy ever finding out about this one. And it doesn't have to be like it was with Tina. It could just be a one-time thing. A brief burst of passion to brighten up my dull suburban life. Then I will leave it. I will return to my wife, and Petra will move onto the next lucky guy to catch her eye.

Nobody has to know except the two of us. Amy doesn't have to get hurt this time because I will make sure of it.

The only question now is how do I see Petra again? She definitely can't come here. That almost ended in disaster a second ago and I don't want to tempt fate. I also don't want to do anything with another woman in this house. Amy deserves better than that. I have to go to Petra. But where? A hotel room? That feels so seedy. I should know because that's what I did with Tina. What about Petra's place? That could work. I could call around, we could get this thing out of our systems, and then we can move on with our lives. The only problem is that I don't know where she lives.

But Michael does.

I could get it from him. But the issue I have is that I don't want to confront him about still seeing Petra because he will want to know how I found out. I can't risk him thinking that we have been in any kind of contact because Amy might find out and it will send her paranoia into overdrive again.

But if I don't speak to him about it then how else can I get her address?

The answer comes to me in two seconds.

He has her phone number.

I could get it off his phone and text her.

The nervous energy in my body is replaced by the overwhelming wave of excitement about what I am going to do in the future.

I am going to be with Petra.

And nobody is going to find out about it.

THE TENTH LESSON

The plaque was built into the new school wall to remember the victim of the fire. The teacher who had died in the inferno would never be forgotten here. His grieving relatives were present on that sunny day when the ribbon was cut and the school was officially opened again, although his wife was absent after her suicide shortly after the fire took her partner. Also present were prospective pupils, teachers, journalists and even the firefighters who had battled the blaze that had seen the original school burn to the ground. On a site that held so much tragedy, it was a relatively positive occasion. The sky was blue, the air was warm, and everybody present was optimistic about a bright new future for Sharpbell High.

But there was somebody watching from a distance that day who wasn't feeling as hopeful for the future. It was the person who carried with them the guilt from the events on that fateful night when the fire had swept away the classrooms and the corridors and the poor man stuck inside. It was the person who was also feeling remorseful for helping frame the poor girl who had gone to prison for this fire, the same girl who had been killed by a fellow inmate while the building work on this new site was still underway.

It was Amy.

She hadn't caused the fire, but she was far from innocent. She knew who had done it. She also knew that they had gotten away with it.

The tenth lesson is that everybody has secrets.

46

AMY

I can see the gold trim of the plaque from over here. I stare at the section of the school wall while I wait for Bella to come and get in my car so we can get out of here. Another school day is over, and it's one day closer to the day when I never have to come back here again. I've cried enough tears and felt enough remorse over the years for the people who died because of the fire, both directly and indirectly. I'm worn out from thinking about it. I learnt a long time ago that I couldn't change what happened because it's far too late for that. Saying something now won't bring back the teacher, his wife or the poor girl who died in prison. They are gone, and nothing can change that. The families have moved on, the school has moved on, and I have moved on. I was coping. I had put it behind me.

Then I got that photo on my phone.

It was a picture of the dead girl, the one I helped frame for the fire and the one who was strangled to death in her cell while serving the sentence that she should never have been given in the first place. The fact that I received a photo of her tells me that somebody knows what I have done and how involved I was in the whole shameful affair. I've given up wishfully thinking that the photo was some kind of a prank to mark the twenty-fifth anniversary of the fire. It isn't a joke.

It's deadly serious.

I did try ringing the number to try and find out who had sent it. But there was no answer. It's hardly a surprise. They obviously want to keep their identity a secret because they can torment me more that way. But I'm wondering what is going to happen next. Since receiving the photo, I haven't had anything else from this number. No more photos. No message. Just the constant wave of anxiety washing over me again and again and making me feel like I am starting to drown.

Everything seems to be falling apart. Michael is currently serving a suspension from school after being involved in two fights last week. One was during a lunchtime football game, which has been known to happen before and could be put down to kids being competitive and overexcited on the pitch. But the second one was much more troubling.

He had been fighting with Nev.

I have no idea what the two friends were arguing about, but they have never fought before. My son might not be an angel, but he has never thrown a punch at anybody, let alone his own best friend. But he still won't tell me what caused it, nor will he confess the reason as to why he has been so moody lately. Nick suspects that it is because his exams are almost here, but I don't think it is that. Michael has proven that he doesn't really care what happens regarding his schoolwork, so I doubt he is suddenly worried about it now. But it still remains a mystery. At least his suspension ends in time for the exams to start.

As for Bella, she came home with a black eye the other day. The girl who has been bullying her pushed her into a door, and she has been suspended, but that isn't much consolation for my daughter who didn't deserve such a thing to happen to her. But she is bravely soldiering on and still going to her classes, which is at least one less thing to worry about.

That just leaves my husband. Nick has been behaving very strangely lately, and just like my son, I have no idea what is behind it. He's mumbled some stuff about being behind on several deadlines with work, and he has tried to keep himself shut away in his study as much as he can, but I can tell there is something more on his mind. Worst of all, he and Michael have had some barnstorming arguments lately. I don't know what's got into them, but there have been several times when I have heard them going at it with each other. But every time I try and get to the bottom of it, neither of them are willing to give me an answer.

I feel like I am losing my grip on my own life as well as my family's. I've spent the last week trying to figure out why this is all happening now. It's only when I see the school kids stream out of the door beside the plaque that I have a sudden epiphany.

Everything started going wrong when I let Petra go.

The photo on my phone. Michael's misbehaviour. Nick's aloofness. It all began after I changed the tutor.

I feel my breath catching in my chest as I watch the kids pouring out of the school and rushing towards the waiting cars and buses. I feel it because I know it is true.

Petra is behind this. She displayed a cold streak to me that night as she left my home, hinting that she could have had my husband if she had wanted to. That showed me that I had never really known her. There is clearly a lot more to her than the smiling, polite teacher from Sweden. But how much more?

Did she come into our lives for a reason? Did she plan it all? Does she know what I have done?

I take out my phone and open the message with the photo attached.

Then I type out another reply to it, and I am confident that this one will get me a response.

I know it's you, Petra. What do you want?

47

PETRA

I have what I want. He's lying right next to me in my bed.

'I better be going,' he says, reaching for his t-shirt that was thrown onto the bedside table during our fit of passion.

'Stay a little longer,' I say, pulling him back towards me.

I'm not surprised when he doesn't resist. No man could.

We kiss again, and I feel the desire emanating from within him. I wish he could stay the night. But his wife wouldn't like it.

'I really have to get going,' Nick says as he breaks off from the kiss and climbs out of bed before I can pull him back again. I watch him getting dressed and find myself amused that he took his clothes off a lot quicker than he is currently putting them back on.

'When will I see you again?' I ask, even though we have agreed this was only going to be a one-time thing.

'Petra,' Nick starts, but then he sees the grin on my face and realises that I'm joking.

'Don't worry. I won't keep you from her anymore,' I say, but I regret it when I see the wave of guilt flash across his face.

He finishes getting dressed in silence, and I wait for him to speak next.

'What about the other thing we talked about?' he asks when he has his clothes back on to go with the wedding ring that never came off.

'I'll sort it out,' I reply.

'Promise?'

'Yes, I promise.'

He nods. Now he has got what he wanted and his clothes are back on, there isn't really anything else keeping him here.

'I guess I'll be going then.'

I watch him walk to the door, imagining how he will behave when he gets back home to the woman he should have been with all along. I hope that when I get married, I will be able to tell if my husband is lying to me. But maybe I won't. Maybe I'll be just as unfortunate as Amy.

I do feel sorry for her. I know I have a funny way of showing it considering that I have just slept with her husband, but I genuinely do. She doesn't deserve this. And she doesn't deserve what is coming. I'm not even sure Nick does either.

'Wait,' I say just before he can walk out of the bedroom and leave my flat forever.

Nick pauses in the doorway and looks back at me, his eyes moving from my face to my naked torso and the rest of my body concealed beneath the bedsheets.

'Be careful,' I say, even though I shouldn't be saying anything at all.

'What do you mean?'

I almost want to tell him. I want to give him a heads up about the chaos that is coming his way very soon. But I don't. I'll keep my word. I've gone off plan enough. I can't make it any worse. Not that it could get much worse for Nick and his family when we are finished with them.

'I just mean in general. You're a nice guy. Be careful.'

Nick smiles, and I know he would love to dive back between the sheets with me. But he does what he is supposed to. He walks out the door and goes home to his wife.

Better late than never I suppose.

I roll over when I hear the front door click and pick up my mobile phone from where it is charging on the bedside table. That's when I notice that I have one new message.

Look what I just got it says followed by a copy of another message.

I know it's you, Petra. What do you want?

I guess Amy thinks that she has figured it out. But she is still way off. She thinks that I'm the bad guy here, but I'm not. Okay, I just slept with her husband, but that's beside the point. There's more to it than this. There's more to it than me. It's only a matter of time until she learns the truth along with everybody else in this poxy town unless she does what I say.

I type out a reply to the message.

Let me know what you want me to do next...

Then I put my phone back down on the table and stretch my arms above my head. I better think about getting in the shower and washing Nick's scent off me. His son will be here soon for his next lesson, and it wouldn't be good if he knew what I had been doing with his dad before he arrived. Michael is going to be frustrated enough without him knowing his dad has just done to me what he never will. That's because I'm about to break the poor boy's heart.

I'm going to tell him that tonight will be our last lesson together. He isn't to come here anymore, and he isn't to see me again. I'm sure he'll be disappointed. He might even get mad. But he will leave. There is a chance that he refuses to accept it and tries to see me again in future, turning up at my flat and begging to be let inside. But that won't be my problem.

I'll be long gone by then.

48

MICHAEL

Everything is a mess right now. I've fallen out with Dad, I've fallen out with Nev, and I'm probably on the verge of falling out of school if I'm not careful. But there is one thing that is keeping me going. It's Petra. I'm on my way to her flat right now, and I've decided that tonight is going to be the night when I tell her how I feel.

None of the other stuff matters as long as she likes me too. I don't care about what my family will think or what my friends will think, and I definitely don't care about getting to finish school and earning my grades. None of that will matter if we are together.

Everything is meaningless compared to love.

I get off the bus and step out onto the wet concrete, keeping my head down as I walk through the driving wind and rain on what is another typically rubbish day of weather in England. I'm annoyed because I spent time doing my hair before I left the house, but it was a wasted effort. I'm probably going to look like a drowned rat when I get to Petra's flat. Hardly the best start for what I am planning this evening. But what can I do? I don't have a car, and I can hardly ask Mum and Dad to give me a lift here. They don't even know I've left the house. As far as they are concerned, I'm revising in my bedroom, not halfway across town on my way to see my Swedish tutor.

I can't wait to see Petra. Putting to one side how I feel about her, she is actually a better teacher than the replacement tutor that my parents have given me. Sue is so boring. She has no sense of humour and makes no attempt to make the lessons enjoyable. I'm learning even less with her than I am with Petra, which is saying something. All she does is read from the book, word for word. It's hardly teaching.

It's now only a couple of weeks until my exams, and I don't have long left to revise, assuming I haven't been expelled before then. The fight with Nev was regrettable, but we haven't spoken to each other since. He was talking about Petra in a derogatory way, and I defended her, although I could perhaps have done it in a better way than by punching him in the stomach. I just couldn't stand to hear him talking about her like that. She isn't just some hot girl that I fancy, she is a clever, hardworking and talented woman and she doesn't deserve to be spoken about by a bunch of childish schoolkids on the playground. But because it was my second fight in quick succession, it meant I had ended up getting a suspension, which means I haven't been in school this week. I'm due back just before my exams start which hardly seems worth it, but I think that is only because Mum begged the headmaster to let me return in time. It's all been very stressful, and it has made my home life even worse, which was the catalyst for my troublemaking at school in the first place.

I have been arguing with Dad ever since the day I saw Petra leaving our house. I confronted him about it in his study, telling him what I saw and demanding to know what she was doing at our house, but he refused to tell me the truth about why she was there. He had just kept saying it was because the tutor had left a textbook behind after one of my lessons, but I know that is rubbish because the only textbook we used has been at Petra's flat ever since I started going there. She must have been there for something else, but Dad refuses to tell me what. I threatened to tell Mum about it but then he threatened to tell her that I was secretly seeing Petra for private lessons, which came as a shock because that means she betrayed our agreement.

I can't believe she told my dad that she was still teaching me. I'm not sure why she would have done that. But I haven't asked her. I have never mentioned the fact that I saw her leaving my house that day. I'm telling myself it is because I'm an adult and only a child would go snooping in other people's business. But really, it's because I'm worried about what the truth might be.

I'm worried that something has happened between Petra and my dad.

I have carried that jealousy with me for the last few days, and it is the thing that has fuelled so many of my arguments with him even though he doesn't know it. But I can't say anything to Petra. I don't want her to see me as some jealous kid who doesn't trust her. Maybe she does like my dad. So what? He wouldn't do anything anyway because he's married to Mum. But if she likes him, then it's because he is an adult. So that's what I need to be too.

In the end, Dad and I made a deal. I wouldn't tell Mum that Petra was at the house that day and he wouldn't tell her that I had secretly been going to the tutor's flat. So far, I have stuck to my word, and I am assuming he has stuck to his because Mum hasn't stormed into my bedroom yet and had a go at me about it. But things between Dad and I are still frosty.

I caught him looking at my phone the other day when I had accidentally left it in the kitchen. He told me he was checking it to make sure that my texts with Petra weren't inappropriate and straying beyond the teacher-student line, which they don't because Petra barely texts me back. But he should never have been going through my personal property, so we had another argument. Mum must wonder what is going on.

Hopefully, all will become clear soon.

It will become clear if Petra reciprocates the affection that I am going to show her tonight. I am going to tell her that I love her, and I just hope she feels the same. If so, then Mum and Dad are going to find out about it because I don't want it to be a secret relationship. Petra and I are grown-ups. We could get our own place. Maybe we could move to Sweden, and she could show me where she grew up. Maybe I can finally get out of this town and away from Mum, Dad and childish Nev. But before any of that, I have to let Petra know how I feel.

I can see the front door to her flat across the street. The rain is getting harder, and my hair is ruined. But I don't care. I could be seconds away from having all of my dreams come true.

49

AMY

I wish I hadn't sent that text message to Petra. I wish I hadn't said that I thought it was her who had sent me the photo and asked what she wanted. I wish I hadn't done it because she had text me back, or at least I presume it was her.

Now I know what she wants.

And it's worse than I feared.

She wants to make me pay for what happened all those years ago after the fire at the school. She wants to get justice for the people whose lives were ruined that day. And she wants to ruin my family.

She doesn't want much, does she?

I can't deal with this on my own. I need my husband's help. I still haven't shown him the text message that I received but I'm going to do it now.

I knock on the study door and walk in, expecting to see Nick sitting at his desk, working away on his latest I.T. problem.

Instead, I find him lying on the floor doing sit-ups. He seems embarrassed when I catch him.

'Oh hey,' he says, quickly getting to his feet and clearing his throat. But I don't have time to ask why he is suddenly so interested in his figure again. I just show him the message on my mobile phone.

It takes a few seconds for the words to process in his brain, but I know the moment they do because his eyes go wide and he looks up at me with the same expression he has displayed before.

It's an expression of fear.

'Petra sent this?' he asks.

I nod.

'Are you sure?'

'I asked if it was her and she said yes. Who else would it be?'

'There must be a mistake,' Nick says, shaking his head. 'Why would she do this?'

'Because she's crazy.'

'Is she? She's just a tutor.'

'I think it is obvious now that she is so much more than that,' I say, taking back my phone and re-reading the message for what must be the thousandth time since I received it.

'I don't understand. How could she know?' Nick asks, slumping into his desk chair.

'I've no idea, but she obviously does. Did you tell anyone?'

'Of course not. You?'

I gave him a stare so cold that he knows better than to ask me that.

'Okay, it doesn't matter,' he says quickly. 'She knows. But what could she gain from this?'

'That's the thing. She hasn't asked for anything. Not yet, anyway.'

'So what do we do?'

My husband hasn't been much help so far. He is just stating questions that I have already asked myself dozens of times.

'We have to meet with her in person and find out why she is doing this and how we can make it stop.'

'I don't think that's a good idea,' Nick replies, and I don't either, but it's the best one I can come up with right now.

'Any other suggestions?' I ask.

His silence tells me there are none.

'I'll text her and tell her to come to the house during the day when the kids are at school. Then we can find out what all of this is about.'

'Michael will be here,' he replies.

Shit. His suspension. He will be here.

'I'll speak to the school again. I'll beg them to let him come back earlier for the sake of his exams. They owe me one after what one of their pupils did to Bella.'

'There has to be another way,' Nick says, but my mind is made up.

I type out the message quickly and press send.

It's time for Petra to come back to our house.

50

PETRA

This is going to be all over soon. I'll get the money and be on my way, and I'll never have to think about this town or any of the people in it ever again. But first I have to get through this meeting with Amy and Nick.

It's raining again, and it's starting to feel like it hasn't stopped over these past few weeks. That's the last bit of motivation I need to make my way up this driveway and towards the front door of the house where the truth will finally come out. Soon I'll be lying on a beach somewhere with the hot sun on my skin, and this dreary place with its gloomy weather will be a distant memory.

It can't happen quick enough.

I knock on the door and wait for the homeowners to answer. I hope it will be Nick, but I expect it will be Amy. I haven't seen the man of the house since he left my flat having spent an hour in my bed, but I don't imagine it will be too awkward. At least it won't be on my part. I'm not the one who is married after all.

But I am relieved that Michael won't be home. This meeting has been set for 10 am on a Wednesday, which means he should be at school right now, along with his little sister Bella. Amy would never have arranged this meeting for a time when her children were in the house, and I am grateful for that. Now I won't have to see the boy whose heart I broke just a few days ago.

Michael confessed his love for me at my flat during our last lesson, but he didn't take it too well when I told him that I didn't feel the same way. I felt bad for being so brutally honest with him, especially after he had just been the same way with me, but I couldn't give him false hope. He was only ever supposed to be a way into the family for me, and I hate that he is caught up in this because he doesn't deserve that. But I couldn't give him what he wanted, or at least not all of it. I couldn't give him my love.

But I did give him a quick kiss.

I know he wanted so much more but it was the best I could do. It will be one positive thing for him to look back on after this whole sorry mess is over.

The sting of my rejection coupled with the surprise of the kiss meant he had left my flat before I even had a chance to wish him well for his exams. I will be long gone by the time he takes them, but I sincerely hope he does well. There's no doubt it's going to be a struggle for him and the fact I have broken his heart won't have helped matters, but things will work out in the end.

Or at least I told him they would.

I can see movement through the frosted glass of the front door and recognise the silhouette of the person coming to open it. It is Amy, just as I predicted. I imagine that it was her idea to set up this meeting today and I bet that she will be doing most of the talking within it. Nick will probably be very quiet, one because of the subject matter being discussed and two because the woman he just cheated with will be sitting across the table from his wife. But he's not my concern. I'm here to do the last part of my job. Then I get paid and I can leave. Then this fucked up family can sort out their issues on their time, not mine.

The door opens, and Amy and I come face to face.

Neither one of us says hi.

The time for small talk is over.

51

AMY

The three of us sit at the kitchen table. Nick sits with his back to the shelf full of my cooking books. Petra sits opposite him with her back to the kitchen counters that I didn't bother to clean before this meeting. And I sit in between them with my back to the wall because it's the perfect position to sum up how I feel in my life right now.

Nobody has said a word yet, but I'm about to put us all out of our misery.

'What do you want?' I ask the Swedish woman with the annoyingly calm expression on her face.

Petra takes a moment to answer, and it annoys me that she is looking at Nick instead of me as she keeps us waiting. But then she finally turns to look at me and speaks her mind.

'Two hundred thousand pounds.'

I feel a mixed reaction to her answer. My first thought is that thank God she is giving us a way out of this and only wants money. But my second thought is how the hell are we going to pay her that ridiculous amount?

I laugh, more from nervousness than anything else, before looking at my husband. But he's still keeping his eyes on the table rather than on this evil cow who has entered our home and asked us for a small fortune.

'Two hundred grand? You think we have that kind of money?' I say, shaking my head at the naïve woman in my kitchen. 'And there was me thinking that you were clever.'

'I am clever,' Petra replies, and her confidence is unsettling. 'I know you have the money otherwise I wouldn't have asked for it.'

I still feel assured in my original response to her that we don't have it, but there is something about the way she speaks that is making me start to doubt things. I look back to Nick and notice that he is now staring at the tutor for the first time.

'How do you know that?' my husband asks, and I feel a wave of anxiety rushing through me. Why is he asking that? Why isn't he saying the same thing as me? We don't have that kind of money.

Do we?

'You're not the only I.T. whizz in the world,' Petra replies with a sly grin. 'You really should be more careful which clients you take on. They give you access to their computers, but some of them have ways of getting access to yours too.'

Now Nick looks worried and that isn't helping my nerves.

'You hacked into my computer?' Nick asks, sitting forward in his seat and closing the gap between him and the young woman opposite him. It's funny how I used to worry about anything ever happening between the two of them, but I have much more important things to worry about now.

'I didn't,' Petra replies. 'Somebody else did. And they know that you have secret bank accounts with just over two hundred thousand pounds inside them. They also know how you have accrued this money. You've invested in many things over the years. Tech companies in Silicon Valley. Cryptocurrency. And even good old Amazon. And you've made quite the profit. But I'm guessing your wife doesn't know anything about that?'

I hate the woman, but she is right. I had no idea that my husband had been investing in things, and I certainly had no idea that he had been sitting on so much profit.

'Anyway, we know you have the money so just pay up and we will leave you and your sordid little secrets alone.'

Petra takes out her mobile phone and holds it out towards us so that we can see what is on the screen.

It's a bank account.

'You'll transfer the money into this account,' Petra says, her once pleasant accent now like nails down a chalkboard to my fuzzy brain.

'Who is we?' Nick asks, ignoring the bank details that are being flashed in front of his face.

That's a good question. Petra said "we." She isn't working alone.

Who the hell is the other person?

'That's not important,' Petra says, turning her phone screen back towards herself and scrolling onto another app. 'What is important is where they are right now and what they are going to do if you don't pay up.'

Petra turns her phone around again and then we see it. It's a photo of Michael and Bella. They are in their school uniform and standing together on the playground.

'I'm not a bad person,' Petra says as my husband and I continue to stare at the phone. 'But the person who took this photo is, and she is watching your children right now. I can't stop her doing anything to them if you refuse to pay up.'

'You crazy bitch!' I cry as I dive across the table towards the tutor.

I get a fist of her blonde hair in my hand, and I'm just about to try and yank it out of her scalp when Nick pulls me off her.

For a second, I see the fear in Petra's eyes, and I have no doubt that I could take her in a fight right now. But I'm not the one in danger here. My kids are.

'Control your wife Nick,' Petra says as she touches the tender part of her hair that she was almost relieved of. 'You can make all of this go away if you just put the money in the account right now.'

Nick and I share a look, and we both know that we don't need to discuss it.

'I'll go and get my laptop,' Nick says sullenly, and he heads for the study, leaving Petra and I standing across the table from each other.

I want to ask her more questions. I want to know everything that she knows. But I'm scared to learn the answers. She is clearly a lot smarter than us and on a level far beyond simple GCSE Maths.

By the time my husband returns with his laptop, I am sitting down again. The next few minutes go by in a blur of fingers on keyboards and digits on screen until suddenly it is done.

With the money in the account, Petra is ready to leave but not before she has assured us that our children are safe.

Time only seems to return to its normal speed again when I hear the sound of the front door closing behind her.

The tutor has gone.

52

THREE MONTHS LATER

MICHAEL

I stare at the envelope in my hands. Everybody else around me has already opened theirs, but I'm in no rush. I know that I have already failed. I feel like my exams were a disaster. I couldn't concentrate on them. All I could think about was Petra.

All I could think about was that she was gone, and I would never see her again. The results inside this envelope are meaningless to me now that I have lost the thing that mattered. Even a miracle of an A* isn't going to bring Petra back. I knew she was gone when I saw the strangers going into her flat. She moved out, and she didn't even say goodbye.

What a bitch.

'I got a B in English!' Nev shouts beside me, and I look at him and his stupidly excited face.

We're friends again now, which I am glad about. The fight was silly, and the person it was over was definitely not worth it. I was sticking up for Petra, but I shouldn't have wasted my time. I shouldn't have risked losing one of my oldest friends over her, especially when it turned out she didn't give a damn about me.

'What did you get in Maths?' Nev asks me with his face still buried in his results sheets. That's when I look back down at the envelope in my hand and decide to just get it over and done with. If it was up to me, then I would just throw this letter in the bin and go and start a game of football in the park, but I can't do that yet. Mum and Dad are desperate to know my results, and I have promised that I will call them straight away. I better find out what I'll be saying to them.

I take a deep breath and open the envelope.

53

AMY

'To Michael!' I say as I hold my glass of wine out in the centre of the table.

'To Michael!' Nick repeats from his seat beside me, and he clinks his bottle of beer against my beverage.

'Well done bro,' Bella offers begrudgingly, reaching out to make her glass of orange juice touch our drinks.

'Thanks guys,' my son says as he brings his glass of coke into the small circle to complete it.

The waiter is quickly at our table as soon as we are finished toasting Michael's exam results, and we quickly run through our order with him before he gives us a smile and leaves us alone again. I've ordered the salmon and Nick has gone for the steak. Bella has asked for a tofu salad because apparently she is vegan now, and the man of the hour has chosen the burger. We have been to this restaurant many times before and the food has always been excellent, so I know we are in for a great evening. And thank God too because these last few months have been horrendous.

Petra might have left our house that day after taking nearly all of our money, but that didn't mean that life had been able to return to normal right away. There had been much for Nick and I to discuss, or rather argue about, and we had certainly done that. I tried to figure out why he had kept so much money a secret from me in his private bank account, and he tried to figure out how somebody had been able to hack into his computer while he worked on it. And together we both tried to figure out who Petra had been working with.

We had our answers to the first two problems but not the third. Nick had kept the money a secret as a safety net in case I one day changed my mind about forgiving him for his affair and kicked him out of the family home. It's not a good excuse, but he said it was the truth and while I'm good at knowing when he is lying to me, I can also tell when he is being honest. It seems I hadn't been the only one who had been left paranoid after his affair. He was worried about me leaving him and taking everything.

As for the computer hack, a gap in a firewall had allowed a mystery hacker to access his laptop and see everything that Nick was doing on it. That meant they had seen him accessing the secret bank accounts, as well as find out that he had been googling tutors in the area. That is presumably how the plan was formed for Petra to come into our home and get close to us. An I.T. expert that Nick hired told him that the tutor website he had found Petra on had been purposefully set to appear at the top of his search results.

But the question of who else she had been working with was still a mystery, along with how they knew that Nick and I had been involved in the school fire. The two of us have spent all summer trying to figure out how somebody could have known what we had done when we were sixteen, but we still have no clue.

We know how the fire started. We know how quickly it got out of hand. We know that the school was destroyed along with the teacher who had been working late inside it. We know that we panicked and planted the evidence on a girl in our year so that she would go down for the crime instead of us. And we know that the girl was killed by a maniac inmate two years after that.

What we don't know is how the hell does somebody else know all of that?

'So how does it feel to be free of school forever?' Nick asks our son as he unfolds his napkin and lays it across his lap in anticipation of the delicious meal that will soon be served at this table.

'I'm not going to lie. It feels pretty amazing,' Michael replies and we all laugh, except Bella who I know is feeling a little jealous that her brother doesn't have to get up early and put on a uniform every day anymore.

'It won't be long until you get your exam results and finish too,' I say to my daughter, even though she is still four years away from experiencing that momentous day herself.

'I'll get better results than him,' Bella says, jabbing her brother with her fork and Michael winces in pain before snatching it out of her hand and putting it across the table where she can't reach it.

'Be nice to your brother,' I say, shaking my head at their antics in such a posh establishment. 'He worked hard to get his grades, and we're very proud of him.'

'He only got C's,' Bella says in a tone meant to make Michael feel stupid. But I know he doesn't care because he did much better in his exams than he expected to do and it was certainly better than Nick and I could have hoped for.

'It doesn't matter what I got,' Michael says, picking up his drink with a smug grin on his face. 'All that matters is that I don't have to do homework anymore and you do.'

I can't help but laugh at that as I take a sip of my wine, and Nick seems just as content right now with his beer. But Bella is still annoyed.

'It's not just him that worked hard, is it? He wouldn't have passed without his tutors. They did all the hard work, not him.'

I smile because that obviously isn't true. Michael was the only one who could answer the questions on those exam papers so he deserves his fair share of credit, and I'm just about to say that when Bella continues.

'I won't need tutors when I do my GCSE's. I won't need Mum and Dad to pay for me. I won't need Petra and Sue.'

I see the waiter coming towards us from across the room, but that's about all I see before the glass of wine falls out of my hand and splatters all across the table.

Nick's white shirt is suddenly covered in the red liquid before he can jump out of the way in time and everybody in the restaurant has stopped to turn and look at our table, but I don't care. I dropped my wine, and it was an accident, but I'm not interested in the waiter who is now trying to get past me to clear up the mess. All I care about is what my daughter just said because now it has suddenly clicked.

The other person. The one who the Swedish woman was working with. That website was designed to be seen by Nick, and it only featured two profiles.

I turn to Nick because I have to tell him right now. I have to tell him that we didn't get screwed by one tutor.

We got screwed by two.

54

SUE

School is very much like prison.

Towering walls. Drab uniforms. Employees to enforce the rules. And rubbish food. Yep, school really is like prison. I should know because I've been in both. But the places I have been in weren't nearly as nice as the grounds where I photographed Michael and Bella only a few months ago. My school was a dump, and the prisons I experienced during my time as an inmate were even worse. But their school is actually quite nice. Of course, it didn't always look that way.

It didn't look that great on the day it got burned to the ground.

That was the fault of their parents, Nick and Amy. They were the ones to blame for what happened at the school on the night it took a teacher's life, and they are the ones to blame for what happened to the innocent girl who ended up in prison instead of them. I know this because I was the only one in prison who listened to the woman who killed that innocent girl.

I was an inmate alongside that woman at the time she killed that poor eighteen-year-old, and I was her only friend in there. That is why I was the only one she explained her actions to before the prison guards dragged her away. She wanted that girl dead so that the school fire would die with her and stop the real truth from coming out, which was that Nick had started it and his girlfriend Amy had helped him cover it up.

She told me that she had seen Nick and Amy at the school that night and witnessed what they had done. She had also followed them to the innocent girl's home where they had planted the evidence in her garden. The prison killer had been in love with Nick and had been driven by the need to protect him at all costs, ultimately committing crimes just so she could end up in the same prison as the girl her crush had framed. Then she killed her because she thought that was the only way to stop the truth from coming out. She thought she was protecting Nick, even though he barely knew she existed.

Nick knows what happened that night. Amy does too.

But they didn't know they had been seen.

It took a long time for me to finish my sentence and be released into society again, and it took a little while longer to put my plan into action. I had to learn new skills, and I had to hire an assistant. But cyber-crime is the new way of doing things so it was worth learning how to hack somebody's laptop and it sure was better than the type of crimes I had been locked up for in the first place. But things don't always go to plan, which is why it was worth me bringing on an assistant too.

I knew I was going to blackmail Nick and Amy for whatever amount of money they had once I got released, but I enlisted the help of a fellow inmate to be my partner when we were on the outside. That woman was Petra from Sweden or rather, it was Stacey from Solihull. The whole Swedish persona was just something Stacey did for fun after falling in love with the

Scandinavian culture while in prison. She spent months on the inside practising that accent and even I was impressed by how good she became at it. All she had to do when she got out was dye her hair blonde and use teeth whitener and she had suddenly turned into a Nordic goddess.

As for me, after posing as a male client for Nick's I.T. business, I had hacked into his PC and found out exactly how much money I was going to be able to bribe him out of if he wanted his dirty little secret to stay hidden. I was shocked to see he had so much, but I wasn't complaining. Then I had watched his movements on the web and waited for a way in.

I wanted that way in because I needed to get to know Nick and Amy better before I attempted to bribe them. Understanding the psyche of a mark is a crucial step that I had overlooked in my youth, and it had led to most of my earlier attempts at crime failing. I've learnt my lessons after decades behind bars because I had underestimated people or not done my research thoroughly before acting. This time was different. This time I was determined to find a way to get as close to the targets as possible. And I knew it was important to because Amy and Nick weren't just some naïve couple.

I knew exactly what they were capable of.

After a while, I noticed Nick's frequent internet searches for a GCSE tutor and that had been our way in. He had also been searching for cleaners around that time, but I'm glad we could go the tutor route instead. Reading questions out of a textbook is easier than scrubbing toilets, that's for sure.

In order to make sure that Nick and Amy got in touch with me, I had manipulated Nick's search results to show him the site with mine and Petra's fake tutor profiles on and then it had just been a case of at least one of us getting through the door and into their lives. Fake Facebook profiles had been the icing on the cake.

As it happened, we both ended up teaching their son, and we ended up working well as a team together. I paid Petra £20,000 of the total takings, which I know she wasn't happy about at the time we agreed on it, but it's certainly more than real tutor's get paid for a couple of month's work. And I know that she ended up having a little fun with the married man during our scheme because I kept an eye on her too.

I wasn't impressed by what she did with Nick, but then she has spent a lot of time behind bars and missed the company of a man. In the end, she didn't do too badly out of the whole thing. Of course, I did much better, taking £150,000 for myself. The remaining £30,000 was left in a box on the doorstep of the innocent woman's house for her parents to find, which won't make up for the loss of their daughter but at least makes me feel like I have done something to get justice for the deceased.

Now I'm wealthy, free and unburdened by any guilt, which means I can enjoy my cocktail as I sit here and look out over the beautiful blue sea in the Algarve. I imagine Petra is on her own beach somewhere right now doing the same thing. We might meet up again and work another job together, but it will be a long way from Nuneaton, that's for sure.

I don't know what I will do next, but the world is my oyster. I could find myself a rich man, I could do some more travelling, or I could go and get myself a job. But what would I do for work?

I hear being a tutor pays well.

THE FINAL LESSON

There isn't much a teenage couple won't do to be together, but those two sixteen-year-olds went far beyond the line that night. Amy was at the school because Nick was there, and another night of fooling around outside of their parent's homes seemed on the cards. But it wasn't just any old night of teenage tomfoolery.

They had a plan.

They wanted to start a fire.

The jerry can full of fuel that he had stolen from a classmate's house during a party last week would be the way. But the fire quickly got out of hand, and the whole building was soon ablaze. If he had known that a teacher was working late inside, then he would never have done it. But he had no idea. Neither did Amy. They just thought they would cause a little damage and get the school shut down for a couple of days, while also landing a certain classmate in trouble.

In the end, they destroyed several lives with their actions that night.

As the fire took hold, Nick and Amy made sure to leave the jerry can nearby for the police to find. That was important because on the bottom of the can was the address for the girl who they wished to frame for the crime.

It was the girl who had bullied Amy for much of her youth, and after Nick had attended a house party at the girl's house and seen the jerry can, he and his girlfriend had seen an opportunity for revenge. Amy knew that girl was at the local park on the night of the fire, which meant her parents wouldn't be able to give her an alibi. She would be alone after leaving her friends in the park to go home, which provided a window of opportunity that the police would later be interested in. Without anyone to confirm her whereabouts for the whole evening, and already a renowned troublemaker at the school, she could fit the bill as a suspect. The recovery of the jerry can with her parents' address on would make sure she was the only one and the fact that she had been seen walking back from the park that night which was nearby the school also put her in the area where the crime took place.

With that evidence, no other suspects, and pressure from the public for the police to solve the case quickly, Nick and Amy's plan worked.

The young couple had no idea of the severity of the situation that night. If they had done then maybe they would have acted differently. They just wanted Amy's bully to get into a bit of trouble. Maybe get expelled. They never wanted her to be blamed for manslaughter. But by then the school had been burned down, the teacher's body had been found and the innocent girl had been arrested. The teacher's grief-stricken wife killed herself, the people of the town vilified the accused, and the judge felt compelled to not only find the defendant guilty, but to give her a harsh sentence.

Amy and Nick had been bonded by love.

But after that night, they had been bonded by so much more.

Death.

Destruction.

And one dark secret.

The final lesson is that love makes people do crazy things.

THE END

Coming soon from Daniel Hurst

RUN AWAY WITH ME

What if your husband was wanted by the police?

Laura is feeling content with her life. She is married, she has a good home, and she is due to give birth to her first child any day now. But her perfect world is shattered when her husband comes home flustered and afraid. He's made a terrible mistake. He's done a bad thing. *And now the police are going to be looking for him.*

There's only one way out of this. He wants to run. *But he won't go without his wife...*

Laura knows it is wrong. She knows they should stay and face the music. But she doesn't want to lose her man. She can't raise this baby alone. *So she agrees to go with him.*

But life on the run is stressful and unpredictable and as time goes by, Laura worries she has made a terrible mistake. They should never have ran. But it's too late for that now. Her life is ruined. The only question is: *how will it end?*

You can run but you can't hide...

Available February 2021

Join my free mailing list to receive updates about this book, as well as for freebies, competitions and a sneak peek into the life of an author at www.danielhurstbooks.com

Also By Daniel Hurst

The bestselling psychological thriller:

TIL DEATH DO US PART

What if your husband was your worst enemy?

Megan thinks that she has the perfect husband and the perfect life. Craig works all day so that she doesn't have to, leaving her free to relax in their beautiful and secluded country home. But when she starts to long for friends and purpose again, Megan applies for a job in London, much to her husband's disappointment. She thinks he is upset because she is unhappy. But she has no idea.

When Megan secretly attends an interview and meets a recruiter for a drink, Craig decides it is time to act. Locking her away in their home,

Megan realises that her husband never had her best interests at heart. Worse, they didn't meet by accident. Craig has been planning it all from the start.

As Megan is kept shut away from the world with only somebody else's diary for company, she starts to uncover the lies, the secrets, and the fact that she isn't actually Craig's first wife after all...

Available now on Amazon and in Kindle Unlimited

Read on for the first two chapters...

1

MEGAN

The thought of getting out of bed to do nothing all day might appeal to some people, but it's not all it's cracked up to be. I've never considered myself to be a lazy person, yet that seems to be what I've become. How did this happen?

Three words.

I got married.

I don't regret saying 'I Do' to my husband, Craig, but I do regret saying 'I quit' to the only boss I've ever had before. That's because while I have a sparkling ring on my finger, a large home in the country and a loving husband who earns a fortune in the city, I don't have much else.

No children. No friends. No job.

The no children situation is okay because both Craig and I agreed not to have kids before we married. He said he'd never wanted them, and I was happy to say the same, having always doubted I'd be able to pull off motherhood without going insane. My lack of friends is a shame but is unfortunately just what happens when you buy a house at the opposite end of the country from where you were born. But the job situation...

Now that is something that I would like to change.

Craig is the General Manager at the London Branch of a Swiss bank, so money is not an issue for us. His base salary is staggering enough before you factor in the end of year bonuses, which are frankly obscene, but are still gratefully accepted. But the financial security that my husband's job has given us has meant that it was deemed unnecessary for me to work as soon as we were married. Being told at the age of twenty-nine that you could retire and put your feet up might sound like a dream come true to most people, and it certainly was to me when I heard Craig say it, but now I'm thirty-two, and I'm not so sure.

Yes, I have money, but it's my husband's money, not mine. I haven't earned a penny of it, and while he is happy for me to spend a chunk of it each month on nice things for myself and the house, even that's starting to grow old.

I want to make my own money.

I want to have a purpose and a profession.

Most of all, I want to have a reason to get out of bed in the morning.

The sound of Craig's electric toothbrush in our en-suite bathroom is like a buzz saw to my fuddled brain right now. But I'm not tired. I'm the opposite. I sleep too much. Through until noon some days. But not today.

Today I am determined to get up and make the most of all my free time.

Craig will leave the house in about twenty minutes when he has put on one of his expensive suits and chomped down a Granola bar. He will close the front door behind him at 6:10 am before getting in his Porsche and driving to our nearest train station, which is fifteen minutes away, or ten if he opens up the engine on the quiet country roads. I've told him he's not to speed, but boys will be boys. Besides, it's not as if there is ever anybody else out on the road at this time.

We really are in the middle of nowhere.

With Craig out of the house all day, I will be alone again. But instead of browsing retail websites and filling my virtual shopping basket with things that I don't need, I am going to do something productive today.

I am going to look for a job.

It's hardly an earth-shattering thing to do, but I haven't worked for three years, and the thought of putting my CV out there is enough to give me butterflies. But that's not the only thing that I'm anxious about.

I'm not sure how Craig will take the news about me wanting to go back to work.

The toothbrush is turned off, the toilet is flushed, and finally, the bathroom door opens, and I get my first glimpse of my handsome husband today. He's always been a morning person, and his smart appearance is evidence of that. The clock beside the bed is showing 06:06, but my man is up and ready to take on the world, which is more than can be said for me, as I lie beneath the duvet suffering from a bad case of what can only be called 'bed-head.'

"Oh, you're awake," Craig says, obviously surprised to see my eyes open and watching him from across the spacious bedroom. "Sorry, I thought I was quiet."

"That's okay, I want to get an early start today," I tell him, knowing full well he will be intrigued enough to ask why I need such a thing, unless he presumes that there is a sale about to start on one of my favourite retail websites.

"What for?" he asks, putting on his tie and growing more dashing by the minute.

"I was thinking about seeing if there are any good jobs available," I say, nervous to see what the response will be. It's not that he wouldn't want me to work. It's just that he might not understand why I would feel the need to.

"A job?" he replies, pausing as he pulls on his suit jacket. I'd expected him to be surprised. Maybe it's a silly idea.

"I didn't know you wanted to get back into work," he says, now fully dressed and ready to leave. "I thought you were happy not having to go to an office every day."

"I was. I mean, I am. It's just..."

I pause, not wanting to get into it just before he's about to walk out the door. I don't want to make him late. Then he definitely will be speeding.

"It was just an idea," I say, downplaying it a little. "We can talk about it tonight."

Craig smiles and moves towards the bed, leaning over me and kissing me on my forehead. “Whatever you want, darling.”

Then he heads for the door, leaving my heart aching a little at the thought of not seeing him until he returns this evening.

“Have a good day!” I call after him as he leaves, his footsteps thudding down the staircase before I hear the rattling of his car keys from the hallway below.

“See you tonight, love,” he calls up, before opening the door.

For a second, I can hear the sounds of the birds singing in the trees outside, the fields around our home filled with the sounds of nature as another day dawns in our rural retreat.

Then the door slams and there is nothing but silence.

Home alone.

As per usual.

2

CRAIG

I can't believe Megan is thinking about getting a job. I thought she was happy with our arrangement. I make the money, so she doesn't have to. I'm the breadwinner, and she keeps the home fires burning. I go to work. She stays in the house.

That's how it's always been since we got married. It's how I want it and I thought it was how she wanted it too. But I guess I was wrong. Something has changed, and now she is talking about getting a job.

We'll see about that.

Opening the driver's side door on the black Porsche parked outside the house, I hop inside my expensive vehicle and feel the familiar thrill of knowing that I will soon be powering it through the quiet country lanes towards the train station. As I fire up the engine and put the car into reverse, I don't even need to glance at the time on the dashboard because I know exactly what it will be. 06:15. On the dot. I leave at the same time every day, and I arrive home at the same time every day. I like my life to have structure and routine and as few surprises as possible, which is why Megan's admission this morning has me so riled up.

Pushing my foot down on the accelerator pedal, I guide the beast at my fingertips down the quiet road, past the farmer's field opposite my house and in the direction of the small train station where I will catch the 06:32 service into Central London. But my mind isn't on the twists and turns of the route ahead. It's on Megan and her desire to find herself back in gainful employment again.

Most women would be happy if their husband earned a fortune that allowed them to not have to commute every day to a job they loathed. How many people can say they got to retire at the age of twenty-nine because they had somebody willing to take care of them and allow them to enjoy their life, instead of having to spend the best years of it toiling away behind a desk or standing over a photocopier?

I know all about hard work, having left university with a first-class degree and gone into the working world, beginning as a Teller on the cashier desk in a branch of a Swiss bank in Manchester. With my dedication to the role and my willingness to learn, it didn't take me long to become the Head Teller, and after some time spent working abroad in Head Office, I was on the fast-track to the senior level. I was Head of Retail by my late-twenties and head-hunted by the London branch to become the UK General Manager before thirty.

Fast forward three years, and here I am, just thirty-two and already at the top of the food chain in my place of work. Not only that, but I am also the proud owner of a seven-figure home in the Berkshire countryside and a breath-taking black supercar that makes me purr almost as much as the engine does. I have loyal friendships, made in both my childhood and adult life, as well as many hobbies, including football, badminton and squash. And to top it all off, I am married to Megan, the beautiful brunette who caught my eye on a night out in Manchester.

The only thing an outside observer would think I was missing would be children, but that's where they would be wrong. I don't want kids, and I made sure my future wife didn't want them too. Megan is an easy woman to persuade and regardless of whether she did want them or not, I was able to sway her to my viewpoint, and now she believes that children are as unnecessary for a happy life as I do. That means that there isn't anything that I want right now. I have it all, and everything is how I planned it to be.

Until Megan told me she was going to look for a job.

It's not that I don't appreciate my wife's desire to earn her keep and do something more productive with her days than blow a big chunk of my wages on shoes, handbags or another awful cushion for the sofa. It's just that I like to apply the same structure and routine in my life to that of my darling wife and that means knowing exactly where she is and what she is doing at all times of the day. There's a good reason why I made sure to buy a house in the middle of nowhere, a long way from anybody, never mind anybody that Megan might have known before meeting me. It's because I want to keep her at home, not under lock and key, but far enough from anyone else to prevent them from threatening the perfect control I have over my spouse's life.

Megan thinks I told her to retire because I love her and want her to enjoy her life. In truth, it was because she is easier to manage when she is stuck at home all day and utterly dependent on me. But the fact that she wants a job threatens not just the routine I have put in place for her but also the large degree of reliance she has on me.

Her own job would mean her own wage and her own disposable income. It would mean new people in her life and new social events in her diary. Most of all, it would mean she isn't totally and utterly under my thumb.

Not that Megan realises that. She thinks I'm the perfect husband and that she still exercises her own free will in our relationship. How cute. She has no idea.

That is the way that I will keep it.

But the unexpected development this morning means I have some thinking to do as I speed on towards the train station, going much faster than I should be on these roads. Megan would hate it if she knew I was going this fast. Then again, she would hate a lot of things about me if she knew them.

But she doesn't.

I intend to keep it that way.

TIL DEATH DO US PART
Available now on Amazon and in Kindle Unlimited

Also by Daniel Hurst

INFLUENCE

Would you kill for a million followers?

Emily Bennett dreams of being a social media influencer, just like her idols Mason Manor & Ivy Lane. But shortly after Ivy's untimely death she is contacted by a secretive businessman who offers her the chance at the fame and fortune she so desperately craves.

While Emily initially gets to experience the things she has always wanted, it soon becomes clear that her new employer had sinister motives for approaching her and it isn't long before she discovers that the life of her dreams comes with the kind of conditions that are the stuff of nightmares.

Social media isn't life or death.
It's more important than that.

Influence is available now on Amazon and in Kindle Unlimited and is the first book in ***The Influencing Trilogy.***

You can get ***Influence***, ***Influencer*** and ***Influenced*** as a complete 3 book boxset on Amazon and Kindle Unlimited by searching for 'The Influencing Trilogy.'

Also by Daniel Hurst

20 MINUTES ON THE TUBE

The first full book in the bestselling
20 Minute Series

20 Characters. 20 Chapters. 20 interweaving stories.

Here's what readers of the series are saying about it so far:

Wonderfully clever. Some stories interlocked, some did not, but the book was gripping from page one. I devoured it in a day and will be starting another immediately!
Amazon reviewer

The psychological insight was fascinating, the stories were absorbing and the characters were 3D. I absolutely loved it.

Amazon reviewer

The books in this series are an incredibly easy read, you become invested in the lives of the characters so easily and I am eager to know more and more. Roll on the next book.

Amazon reviewer

I am loving these books and the ways the characters are linked. Fantastic series.

Facebook comment

The last chapter made me literally go "Yesss!" out loud! Great stuff!

Facebook comment

Available on Amazon and in Kindle Unlimited

ALL BOOKS BY DANIEL HURST

THE 20 MINUTES SERIES (in order)

20 MINUTES ON THE TUBE
20 MINUTES LATER
20 MINUTES IN THE PARK
20 MINUTES ON HOLIDAY
20 MINUTES BY THE THAMES
20 MINUTES AT HALLOWEEN
20 MINUTES AROUND THE BONFIRE
20 MINUTES BEFORE CHRISTMAS

INFLUENCING TRILOGY (in order)

INFLUENCE
INFLUENCER
INFLUENCED

STANDALONE PSYCHOLOGICAL THRILLERS

TIL DEATH DO US PART
THE TUTOR

About The Author

You can join Daniel Hurst's mailing list at www.danielhurstbooks.com

You can connect with Daniel on Facebook at www.facebook.com/danielhurstbooks or on Instagram at www.instagram.com/danielhurstbooks

He is always happy to receive emails from readers at daniel@danielhurstbooks.com and replies to every one

Thank you for reading!

Daniel

Printed in Great Britain
by Amazon